GUNS AT C____S

MERLE CONSTINER

SAGEBRUSH
Large Print Westerns

First published in the United States by Ace Books

First Isis Edition
published 2016
by arrangement with
Golden West Literary Agency

A catalogue record for this book is available
from the British Library.

ISBN 978–1–78541–223–3 (pb)

Published by
F. A. Thorpe (Publishing)
Anstey, Leicestershire

Set by Words & Graphics Ltd.
Anstey, Leicestershire
Printed and bound in Great Britain by
T. J. International Ltd., Padstow, Cornwall

This book is printed on acid-free paper

CHAPTER
ONE

It was two minutes after nine when Stiles Gilmore got off the train in southern Idaho, at the little chocolate brown station with its lamplit sign, *Prentiss Creek*. The October night sky above him was rose-purple with a big moon, and the air was crisp and clean with an edge to it, an early warning of the winter to come. It would be some time before they felt that edge back home, back in Texas. Across the darkness of the road, he could see a broken strip of lights, the town's main street. He was a short, big-chested man, thirty-two, knotted and veined and tendoned from hard work. He was a little bowlegged from rundown boot heels plus the lifelong mould of a saddle. Most of the time his eyes were serene, and so thoughtful they seemed fixed, almost blind. His clothes were those of a cowhand.

He picked up his valise, new, bought for the trip. It held nothing but clothes, his razor, and his gun. He expected to be in town for a short time only, a few days. When he returned to this station, the valise would be carrying twelve thousand in gold coins, and he would be carrying the gun. He left the platform, and crossed the road.

1

His clothes were shabby, and had always been shabby as far back into his boyhood as he could remember, because all his life his mind had been on more important things, cows for instance. The fact was that he owned the biggest spread in his county, and one of the most famous in his state, the JJ.

He had owned it for only a year. And that was why he was here, giving an old established JJ customer his best personal attention.

Back home, when he was twenty, he had owned his first small ranch, and by the time he was thirty he owned three. They were mighty small, and widely separated, true, but profitable. Then he got the big idea, and swung the deal. He sold out and bought the famous old JJ, Eastern owned. It had required a back-breaking mortgage, but it looked now like it was going to succeed. Things were still mighty tight, but the danger seemed past.

Last spring a buyer for a Prentiss Creek outfit up here, the Q Cross, had come down to JJ, made a range inspection, and signed a contract for eight hundred prime head, at fifteen dollars, Idaho delivery. The buyer's name was Rush, and he really knew his cattle. JJ records showed he had been doing this for four years.

Stiles' sixty-year-old foreman, Billy Goodhue, who had been with him through thick and thin, was trailbossing the herd north. Telegrams sent back on its progress said it was moving along on schedule. It should arrive here in Prentiss Creek in four or five days. Stiles had come ahead to receive it. It seemed like a sociable thing to do for Q Cross. Sometimes herd shippers, wanting to go out of their way to be friendly, did this. Besides, there was almost a legend in Texas about the hell-for-leather syle of stock business in Idaho, and he was secretly curious to see how true it was.

When he came onto the main street with its yellow windows facing the tracks, he saw that it was composed of frame buildings, of one and two stories, warped and un-painted, and gapped here and there by vacant lots knee-high in dead weeds. Each storekeeper or office occupant or saloonkeeper had laid down his own boardwalk, for his particular building alone, and there would be a shelflike plank walk before five stores, say, and then a step down to a dirt path, and then, perhaps, a single store with its wooden ledge, and then again the path, and so on down the line. Back from this main street, at intervals, ran short side streets, like the broken teeth of a comb. These side streets looked like sections of road, and were of rutted earth, of double-wagon width. Down the side streets would be the corrals and livery barns, probably; and still farther down, the bulk of the town's residences. Or so Stiles imagined.

As he walked, he tried to figure just what kind of a town he was in.

It seemed to him battered and stark and windswept, but he saw nothing, really, to make him think it was especially hardcase.

He had gone a short distance when he came to a corner, and saw, about forty feet down a side street, a sign sticking out from a building and lighted by a lantern on an iron hook. The sign said, *Rooms*, and was decorated by a painted horseshoe and a four-leafed clover. Stiles turned and walked toward it.

When he came to the building's face, he saw another sign lettered across its window, *Beer & Billiards*. He hesitated, then entered. It wasn't exactly the sort of place he'd had in mind, but he put it down to the customs of the country. He'd never considered beds luxuries. However bad the bed proved to be, he knew he had slept in worse.

And worse hotels, too, for that matter. They didn't get much meaner than some of the places he knew back in Texas. Say some of those outlaw hangouts around Paris.

Inside, he found himself in a small tawdry lobby, half papered with magazine illustrations of horses, dogs, and fat chorus girls, plastered to the yellow pine walls with flour and water paste. There was a short counter with a lamp and a homemade checkerboard on it. Behind the counter, the proprietor, a gaunt red-eyed man, was playing checkers with a cowboy in front of him, a big man in bearskin chaps, who was so hairy it almost looked like he had chaps on his arms. The pieces on the board were buttons, all kinds, overcoat, shirt, fly, just about every kind you could think of, but they apparently knew them well, and didn't get mixed up. They were so absorbed, they ignored Stiles and his valise. On the wall behind the proprietor hung a rack of keys, and by the end of the counter rough timber stairs led upward.

By Stiles' left hand was an open doorway to the poolroom, and from here came curses, the snick of balls, and the reek of urine and beer.

It was worse than he had expected, but he put it down to Idaho and said, "Got a room for the night? And how much?"

The proprietor dragged a register from beneath the counter. "One night, one dollar. Was you aiming to be around long? The longer you stay, the cheaper it gits."

"We'll see," said Stiles. He signed the register and laid a silver dollar on it.

He had come on impulse, knowing Q Cross would be flattered by this personal attention, but he had come unannounced. If Idaho was like Texas, people didn't care too much for things that happened unannounced. Long days on the train he had had plenty of time to send word ahead, telegrams saying he was on his way, but somehow it didn't seem too important. Now he wondered.

Rush, the buyer, had mentioned the fact that he didn't live out at the Q Cross, but right here in Prentiss Creek. At this season of the cattle year, he wouldn't likely be out on his trips, but right here, at home.

Stiles decided to pay him a courtesy call, now.

This might take the edge off his showing up so abruptly.

He said, "How do I find a man here in town, a Mr. Rush who works for Q Cross?"

"You a friend of his'n?" asked the proprietor, suddenly expansive.

5

It was funny, Stiles reflected, how the fact that he even knew anybody in town served as a sort of introduction.

"He stayed a week with me in Texas," Stiles said.

"What part of Texas?" asked the hairy cowboy.

The questions were getting a little too specific. They were still on the right side of good taste, but crowding up to being personal. This was natural, and it was natural, too, for Stiles to automatically evade.

He said, "The middle part of Texas." That was vague enough. Texas had a mighty big middle.

The rooming-house proprietor said, "Mr. Rush. Go two blocks west on Main Street, then turn left and go three blocks more. Them last blocks may be a little hard for a stranger to count, what with a few fields and all, but you can tell the place by its two chimneys."

"Thanks," said Stiles. "It's almost nine-thirty. Will he still be up? I wouldn't want to break into his first-sleep."

"Oh, he'll be up," said the proprietor. "Sometimes he shows a light as late as eleven."

"I've saw it even later," said the cowboy. In Prentiss Creek, Stiles decided, you were part of everybody's business.

As Stiles started for the door, the proprietor said, "No need to lug that valise along with you. I'll keep it for you. It'll be safe here."

Stiles came to a halt. This presented a little problem; ordinarily, of course, he would have left it without a second thought. But at the moment, the valise held his gun, and his gun wasn't just any gun. It was the

6

stag-handled .45 given to him by his uncle when he was twenty-one, and was as much a part of him as the fingers were to his hands. It was so important to him, to his way of life, that he couldn't even bear to think of himself without it.

And if he opened his valise and put it on, here and now, and left the valise, it would look mighty strange. Like he was a gunfighter, getting rigged for a trip through the town, or something.

"Thanks just the same," he said. "I'll take it along."

They looked blankly polite.

Stiles returned to Main Street.

As he walked west, now in lamplight as he passed shops and saloons, now in shadow as he passed vacant lots, he saw a glimmering of late activity, and this surprised him, until he realized that some of the outlying ranches would be into their autumn shipping roundups. He went two blocks, and then turned up a side street, as he had been directed.

This street, broad and rutted and deserted, was without sidewalks. It was without illumination, too, except for the big moon overhead, which glazed the buildings he passed in green-silver and indigo. Soon the buildings thinned. He passed the fence of a commercial corral, and a lumberyard. He was just passing a hideyard when a cheerily tipsy voice hailed him from behind.

"Why, it's old Stiles Gilmore!" it called. "What you doing up here so far from home? Hold on, wait a minute."

Stiles stopped, and turned, and dimly saw the man about thirty feet behind him — and threw himself to the earth almost as the man shot.

The man, seeing that he had missed, wheeled and ran. Instantly, he was engulfed in the blackness of the lumberyard.

It was a long time before Stiles forgot the picture, the dim form in the moonlight, right hand straight out from its shoulder, pistol leveled, right forearm braced by the left hand, in the stance of a target competition. Staking everything on a single shot, playing to win, shooting to kill.

As he arose, Stiles opened his valise and buckled on his gun belt. He felt plenty foolish doing it. It was like locking the barn afterwards. By now, he was sure, the man was long gone.

If this was Idaho style robbery, kill your man first, it was pretty rough.

Now that Stiles thought it over, he realized the whole thing had been carefully worked out. The man had hailed him to stop him, so he would make a better target, and turn him around, so that the man could nail him from the front. Shot from the front — even that had been manipulated. Say the gunman had been caught in the act by a citizen; he could always have said that Stiles threatened him, that, in the dark, he couldn't see that Stiles was unarmed. That he had shot in self-defense.

Stiles continued on his way. Residences thinned, fields increased. After a bit he came to a house with a chimney at either end. Boxlike, it had possibly two rooms, and the planking on its sides ran up and down, not crosswise, from ground to eaves, in a fashion favored by some old-timers. Stiles swung from the road, went down a path matted with dead wiry grass, and knocked on the door.

Rush answered immediately. He was a man in his middle fifties, with pouchy jaws and weak eyes. He was so quiet and self-effacing that back in Texas Stiles had found him a good guest; you hardly knew he was around. When he recognized Stiles on the doorstep, he smiled a little, which Stiles had learned to interpret as enthusiasm, and invited him in. Stiles entered.

Almost before he realized it, Stiles had been seated in a comfortable chair by the embered fireplace, with a whiskey glass thrust into his hands. The place was neat, self-contained, efficient. Bed, table, two chairs, and a buffalo robe on the floor. An open door at the back of the room showed a section of scrubbed kitchen. Rush, standing, leaning on a corner of the mantel, grinned fondly. Stiles told him why he had come.

"I decided to be here when the herd arrives," he said. "I want to be at Q Cross and hand it over to Mr. Le Queux myself. I want to be sure he's absolutely satisfied."

"Well, he'll be pleased," said Rush. "I can tell you that. You've got the makings of an enterprising young stockman, and it's my guess you'll go far."

After a moment, chuckling a little, Rush said, "Do I know you well enough to make a personal suggestion?"

"Go right ahead."

"That gun you're wearing. You won't need that up here. This isn't Texas. This is peace-loving, law-abiding country. You'll see a good many guns being worn around here, of course, but mainly by showoffs, or troublemakers, or strangers. And there's something else, too. Southern Idaho gets a good many drifting gunmen and gunfighters floating through, and flaunting a gun could easily be taken as a challenge." Amused, yet at the same time serious, he added, "You'll be happier without it."

"I'll be happier with it," said Stiles, and told him of the attack he had just been through.

Rush listened. His eyes didn't look weak and watery now, they smouldered with indignation and intelligence.

He said, "How did this man know your name?"

"I had just wrote it out for him," said Stiles. "In the register at the rooming house."

"You mean he was standing by your elbow?"

"It could have been. There was one there. Or he could have walked in right after, from the poolroom."

Rush looked at the valise by Stiles' foot on the hearthstone. Big, shiny, new. "I guess that's what he was after."

"Well, he almost got it."

"There's scum hereabouts," said Rush, changing his peace-loving, law-abiding story, "who would kill a man for a package of cigarette papers." He looked cold and harsh as he spoke.

"They got them like that everywhere, I guess," said Stiles.

10

"Where are you staying?" asked Rush.

Stiles described the rooming house.

"That's Shaw's," said Rush. "It's not too bad, I suppose, for an out-country town like this. But most stockmen prefer the Minton House. Listen, why don't you move in with me? I'll get down my camping cot out of the loft."

"I don't think I'd better," said Stiles. "But thanks."

He got to his feet and Rush went with him to the door. As they stepped out into the night, Rush said, "Have you been out to Q Cross?"

"I'm going in the morning."

"When you registered at Shaw's," said Rush, "you remarked there was a man standing by your elbow. I know this terrain and its denizens pretty well. Would you care to describe him? It's very possible I could be of some help there."

"That's all right. Forget it."

"Forget it?"

"If he was the man that shot at me, and I got a good notion he was, then I'll take care of it myself, on my own. That's the way I always choose to do things."

When Stiles got back into the lobby of the rooming house, the proprietor was still playing checkers, but now with himself. When he saw Stiles, he took a key from the rack behind the counter, lifted a flap, and came out. He said, "Have a nice visit with your friend, Mr. Rush?"

"Yes," said Stiles.

They stared at each other a moment, each poker-faced.

"This way," said the proprietor.

They went up the rough timber steps, came out into a hall floored with greasy matting, and entered a room. The proprietor lit a lamp and handed Stiles his key. When he was alone, Stiles locked the door. He slept that night with his gun under his blanket, by his knee, Texas emergency style. That night, nothing happened.

He slept fitfully and awoke uneasy.

Sometime, during a moment of half-sleep in the night, an idea had come to him that the robbery attempt he had gone through hadn't been a robbery attempt at all, but an assassination attempt, pure and simple. And the idea came to him, too, that in some way it was related to his herd. He couldn't work it out so it made any sense, but the feeling grew on him.

His worry over the herd became intense. Had something already happened to it?

He picked up his valise, left the room, and went down the hall and steps, into the lobby. A different man was behind the counter. Stiles passed over his key, said he wouldn't be back, and went out of the building, to Main Street.

Now, in daylight, he got his first good look of the place. A bleak dusty town, in a bleak dusty prairie. Along the northwest horizon was a smoky green film — mountains.

He crossed the road to the tracks and entered the railroad station. The stationmaster in a green eye shade and brown-paper dust sleeves sat at his telegraph key, receiving, writing down the clickety-clack on a pad. Stiles introduced himself and said, "I should have stopped in last night. Did a telegram come for me?"

"One come in last week, sent hold," said the stationmaster. He riffled through a sheaf of papers, selected one, and handed it over.

Stiles read it. It was from his trailboss.

Herd looking fine coming along smooth as silk but country mighty rough. Will arrive Q Cross about two weeks later than our estimated date. Reserve a beer for me up there. Billy Goodhue.

"That's the way it is with a trail herd," said the stationmaster. "Sometimes they're late."

"Right."

"And sometimes they're early."

Stiles nodded, his mind on other matters. So they looked fine, and everything was all right.

"But oftener late than early," said the stationmaster.

"What's that?" said Stiles. "Oh, yes. Right again. How do I find the Minton House?"

The stationmaster told him.

CHAPTER
TWO

After a light breakfast at a cafe, Stiles swung through the double glass doors of the Minton House. The lobby was coming astir for the day, and the place, attractive, scrubbed, respectable, was a long way from Shaw's. A tranquil looking clerk in brass-rimmed spectacles greeted him at the desk. Stiles registered, handed over his valise, and paid for a week in advance. He asked, "How do I find Q Cross?"

"Stranger to this country?"

"Yes."

"This is one of the most unusual parts of Idaho. You shouldn't travel it blind. Would you mind if I gave you a general picture of the vicinity?"

"I'd appreciate it," said Stiles.

"Those mountains you saw outside to the northwest are the Boises, and they're real mountains, not foothills. Our town here is set on the southern edge of what is known as Little Camas Prairie. Little Camas Prairie flows north, past the mountains, and eventually, a hundred miles and more away, joins Big Camas Prairie, but that's out of our picture. You head for the mountains, skirt along them, and after a while come to a broad valley-like gap on your left. Inside that gap is a

14

big pocket of the richest grass that ever grew. That's Q Cross."

"Prairie and mountains north of us," said Stiles. "What's south of us?"

"Four miles south of us is the Snake River, running roughly east and west."

"And what's south of the Snake?"

"Nothing. One of the meanest semi-arid deserts in the world. Hell. Maps call it the Broken Lava Plateau."

"I'll be needing a horse," said Stiles. "What stable in town would you recommend?"

"We keep a small one of our own," said the clerk. "Mainly for our guests. It's a good one." He pointed. "Go down that passage and out the back door. You'll find yourself in a little courtyard. The stable is across the court, facing you. Your room number here will be 12. I'll take your valise. You'll be needing provisions. I'll tell the kitchen to get some together in a grain sack and send them out to the stable immediately."

The Minton House certainly was a long way from Shaw's.

"Thank you," said Stiles.

As he started to walk away, the clerk said to him, "Watch yourself. It's mighty lawless back in there. More people go into that gap than come out of it."

Inside the Minton House Stable, Stiles saw that it was cleaner than most, and offered a small but exceptionally high-quality string of mounts to select from. He explained the trip he had coming up to the stable boss, and chose a fine big black with a wise alert eye. Her name was Cindy. While she was being saddled, the hotel clerk came in through the courtyard door, up to where Stiles was standing; with him was a ferocious looking little man with a ragged gray moustache and a spot of red sunburn on each of his high cheekbones. He waited for Stiles to nod to him, to acknowledge his presence, and when Stiles did so, nodded almost imperceptibly in response.

"This is Mr. Killigrew," said the clerk. "I've known him for four years, and think mighty highly of him. He ranches up in the north, near the very place you're headed for, and is bound there now. I was just mentioning you to him. He says he'll be glad to guide you, for the pleasure of your company."

Stiles thought quick, but answered slow. The man seemed more than adequately endorsed. Besides, Stiles had liked him on sight. He said, "I wouldn't want to put him out."

"You wouldn't put me out none," said Killigrew, satisfied with the courtesy of the answer. "And I always take a special shortcut, through the mountains."

Soon, with no further conversation, Stiles' provisions were tied behind his cantle, Mr. Killigrew was mounted, and they were on their way.

As the town diminished to a speck in the luminous haze behind them, the bleak prairie rolled away from them on all sides. They ate lunch together, amiably, but almost wordlessly, and all afternoon it was more of the same — bunchgrass, bromegrass, and distant dust. After a bit they rode through low scattered hills, topped with lush emerald pines. The land roughened, and by sunset the mountains were upon them, looming over them in the dusk like gray granite fangs.

They camped beneath an eroded overhang of rock.

After a supper of cold cornbread and hard-boiled eggs, donated by the Minton House, with hot bacon and coffee, Killigrew offered Stiles cigarette papers and his little muslin sack of flake tobacco. When Stiles was relaxed, his cigarette going from a coal from the fire, Killigrew said sociably, "I don't want to be personal, but don't you wear that holster a little low for a respectable man?"

"It's all in what you call respectable," said Stiles, amused.

"You ain't on the warpath? You don't have something agin Mr. Le Queux, and are headed for Q Cross to have it out with him? I wouldn't want to have no part in that."

"No," said Stiles. Considering a moment, he said, "I own the JJ down in Texas. Mr. Le Queux is buying a sizable herd from me. This is a business trip."

"The JJ? Them cows is mighty highly esteemed hereabouts."

Stiles took this as an honest comment, and he answered it honestly, without false modesty. He said, "We work all the time, trying to improve the strain."

"I never seen a JJ cow, but from what they say, you sure do it."

"What am I going to find when I get to Q Cross?"

"You're going to find a mighty prosperous little spread. A little on the hard side, maybe, but them's the times. Maybe we'd all be as prosperous if we

17

boiled it down to a business like they do. Some people don't like Mr. Le Queux because he's got a heart like a hungry wolf. He ain't exactly like an ordinary cowman, but he makes it pay off, don't he? It's him, not us, who is buying choice cows from you down in Texas. And most of us would give a lot to be able to afford JJ cattle."

They talked a little more, and before they went to sleep they had laid down the beginnings of a firm friendship.

Early next morning they started their way into the mountains, first weaving their way around masses of rocky rubble, and then, about eight o'clock, beginning their ascent.

It was difficult from the beginning, starting with a dense stand of dry aspen and hawthorne, tilted up before them, and going suddenly into bare outcrop and caprock. Twice they stopped to blow their horses. A serpentine crevice appeared before them, climbing up the mountain, and they fought their way up it, loose shale clattering and sliding beneath their horses hooves. At noon they came out to a broad, grassy shoulder, and stopped to eat a little cold food.

Some distance behind them a clump of lodgepole pines, through which they had passed, and, as they ate, a bird materialized from the treetops, as though caught in an updraft, and flew circling away.

"You see that?" said Killigrew mildly. "That's a woodpecker. He ain't afeared of hawks, and he ain't afeard of mountain cats. He just goes around to the other side of his tree trunk and waits, quiet, until they pass."

Stiles waited.

"But he's afeared of man," said Killigrew. "They's someone yonder."

"I know," said Stiles quietly. "I think he's been on our trail for some time. Back in that rocky crevice, I thought I heard a little clink of loose shale behind us."

"This ain't a common trail," said Killigrew. "In fact, if you'll excuse me, I always call it the Killigrew Trail. Let's wait right here until he catches up with us."

"I'm afraid he won't catch up with us," said Stiles. "If he's been rattling shale and scaring woodpeckers so have we, and he knows we're ahead of him. He hasn't tried to catch up with us yet, has he?"

"Last night I got the idea you were trouble," said Killigrew. "And I got the same idea now, but somehow I don't much care. I hate to admit it, but I've growed to like you. What should we do? Lay up behind a boulder somewheres, and shoot off his ears when he comes into sight?"

"I don't want to get you hurt," said Stiles.

"Don't worry about me. You know who he is?"

"I think I do. I think he's the one who took a shot at me last night, and missed."

"Why didn't you shoot back?"

"I didn't have time to get my gun out of my valise."

The old man laughed so hard he choked. Stiles laughed, too.

"Wait until I tell my wife where Texans carry their guns," said Killigrew.

"But I got it out now," said Stiles. "And it looks like it's going to stay out. What were we intending to do before this came up?"

"Cross the ridge up yonder, and then start down. A short distance down on the other side we come to a place where we was going to separate. I was going to give you instructions."

"We go on to that place," said Stiles.

The place, when they came to it, proved to be a nest of mountain springs, the headwaters of a tiny stream, scarcely a span wide, which flowed to the left, down the slope. Here, Killigrew told Stiles, they were at the edge of the timberline. The air was deathly still but for the whisper of water.

"Here we was going to part," said Killigrew. "But I've changed my mind. I'm going with you to Q Cross."

"No," said Stiles.

"Better yet, you come home with me. I got good friends."

"No," said Stiles. "We're going through this as planned." He hesitated. "You don't think I'm wrong? That you could be in any danger yourself?"

"Not unless it was a robber, and hide and tallow I ain't worth a dollar. He's after you."

"Then that's that," said Stiles. "How do I go?"

"I go to the right, you go to the left. You just follow this little stream. After a bit it and other streams forms a little lake. A bigger stream comes out of this lake on the east, and then you follow this bigger stream. It'll take you right to Q Cross, almost up to the ranch house."

"That doesn't sound too hard," said Stiles.

"You must be a flatland man."

They didn't say goodbye. They didn't even raise their hands in farewell. They smiled at each other stonily, Killigrew twitched his rein. And soon he was gone.

CHAPTER
THREE

Stiles, expressionless, sat his saddle for a minute, and thought it over.

The man behind him was pursuing him, he knew, and after his life, just that and nothing else.

And when, unseen, you were chasing a man in the mountains to murder him you had all the advantages your way. He must know Killigrew, and the Killigrew Trail, and know, too, where Stiles was heading. He had been tagging along, waiting for this minute, waiting for Stiles and Killigrew to separate. Waiting for Stiles to be alone.

The way Stiles saw it, his problem was this. Should he turn to the attack, circle, lay in wait, and shoot the man from his horse, or should he press on and watch himself? Actually, he had no proof of anything. If he should kill the man, and the man was actually innocent, just a wandering cowpoke, say, then that would be terrible.

He decided to press on to Q Cross, to follow Killigrew's directions, using every guile he had ever learned, and get the hell out of this craggy deathtrap as soon as possible.

He touched his mare with his knee, got her into motion, and started down the bank of the tiny stream. He had hunted down men in his day, but this was the first time he had ever been hunted himself. It didn't make him nervous, but he sure didn't like it.

Following the stream, he went down an open space of shale terraces, where the water fanned from shelf to shelf, came abruptly into sparse tamarack growth, and decided he was below the timberline. Wherever he had the chance, he urged on his mare. She made such good time, and she was so surefooted, that he became certain that she was mountainwise. He passed through a belt of fantastically dwarfed firs, and then a broad area of a burnover, caused doubtless by lightning years ago, charred skeletons of ghostly upright trees, and came abruptly into the forest.

It was about noon, and the sun was overhead, but there was no sunlight here, only a watery green twilight filtering down from high foliage which formed a canopy thirty feet overhead. In every direction, the great columnar tree boles extended to the edge of his vision. The stream here was fast becoming a small creek, deeper, with grassy undercut banks, baring tangles of roots, and the forest floor was carpeted with murky ferns and moss.

He had heard or seen nothing behind him. His pursuer knew this country, he decided, and had picked a particular place for the execution.

All at once, like the raising of a curtain, he was out of the forest, and on the banks of the lake. A mule deer, drinking, whisked up before him and vanished.

He had heard of these high-mountain lakes, small, pocketed, some of them never seen by the eyes of man, many almost impossible to find. This one was incredibly beautiful; to Stiles, raised in dusty chaparral and mesquite, it was a delight. Deep cobalt in color, its surface shimmering in a haze of coolness, it was locked in a circular jungle of dense lodgepole pines.

He halted his mare, and, always listening behind him, took his bearings. At first the southern shore, the point where the large stream was to emerge, the stream he was to follow to Q Cross, seemed precisely like the rest of the bank. Then, in the greenery, he saw a thinning of the foliage and knew that was where the stream flowed out, that was where he was headed. Keeping out of sight, within the shelter of the pines, he started his circle of the left bank.

He covered about a quarter of the distance, when he heard a voice call out behind him, "I don't see him. He musta been here and gone."

Stiles backed his mount a little further into the undergrowth and froze.

Through a small break in the bush, he could see the bank near where he had just been.

A man stood on the bank, his hands on his hips, scanning the shoreline. It was the squat hairy man with the bearskin chaps, whom Stiles had seen the night of his arrival at Shaw's; his bridle was looped through his elbow, and behind him stood his horse. Once more he called. "He don't stand no chance. Let's move."

There were *two* of them.

24

The second sat mounted a short distance from his companion, partly in the half-light, partly in the blanket of shadows. He was a lean-looking man, middle sized, and that was all Stiles could tell about him. He wouldn't know him again, nor would he know his horse from its color. He sat with a rifle across his saddle horn, at the ready, and Stiles had the feeling that this could probably well characterize him, always at the ready. The man in the bearskin chaps swung into his saddle, danced his horse, and the two men disappeared into the bracken and brush, around the lake's right bank.

Stiles waited twenty minutes, then retraced to where they had been.

Patiently and thoroughly, he studied the tracks left by their mounts. He had learned the craft in his boyhood from Apaches, who could even tell a mare's sign from a stallion's. When he had finished his study, his mind knew eight horseshoes, but only one did he try to remember. The hind calk on the left hind hoof of the stranger's horseshoe, worn and nicked, left an impression of two dents in the hard earth. He would never forget the size and shape of those dents.

A little later he saw the two men appear on the south bank, and thresh through the undergrowth, down the stream.

With two antagonists on a rocky trail instead of one, the odds against him had not just doubled, but had increased a hundred fold. Two men, in ambush, say, would be a lethal obstacle, one foolish to chance.

He abandoned the route suggested by Killigrew, that of following the stream, and decided to make a wide circle, and then head generally south. If he could find prairie, he could find Q Cross. The important thing was to stay alive and get there. First things first. But second things, he decided coldly, thinking of the man in the bearskin chaps and his companion, certainly second.

He started his loop due west. The pines thinned, and after a bit he came out on a bench. Below him he had an unobstructed view of a plain, generally egg-shaped, enclosed by mountains, with a gap at its eastern end. He could see tiny buildings and a stream, and was sure this was Q Cross. He moved on, crossing the bench and coming out into a small virgin mountain meadow. Beyond the meadow the slope fell roughly through serrated razor-edge ridges; finally, there came another forest, yellow pine this time, and yellow pine meant lower altitudes. By mid-afternoon the last foothill was behind him, and he was out on the plain. According to his calculations, Q Cross lay east. He headed roughly east.

Soon, across the grassy flatland, he saw a line of cottonwoods, and knew this indicated a creek. The ranch house would be on that creek.

When he rode into the Q Cross ranchyard, he was surprised and interested. The spread had a ranch house, barns, sheds, blacksmith shop, corral like any other ranch, but there was a different feeling about them. Stiles immediately placed it as prosperity. First the ranch house. It was a jumble of three cabins built together, each obviously of different age, as though business had been steadily improving. Where most ranches had one barn, or two small ones, Q Cross had two spick and span big ones. Most ranches got by with an open-faced leanto blacksmith shop; here the shop, with its tin roof, was of good dressed lumber. It's corral, too, was of dressed poles. Not fancy or show-off, but efficient, and useful, and well used. Stiles decided Mr. Le Queux was a good stockman, doing well, who knew how to turn back part of his profits into improvements. And that, Stiles' father had always told him, showed intelligent ranching.

The cabins that formed the ranch house were built one in front and two in a row at the back, forming a short stubby T. The cabin in front was the newest, and had a little roof supported by wooden stanchions, making a pleasant little shady veranda. The cottonwoods and the creek lay maybe a hundred yards behind the house.

A man sat on the veranda, by the front door. He sat at ease, in a big wicker fan-backed chair which must have come from New Orleans, and seemed at first to be dozing. He wasn't dozing though, Stiles saw as he came to a stop before the hitching rack; he was squinting, the better to see Stiles against the background of brassy sun. He was neither friendly nor unfriendly, in fact, hardly seemed to exist, until Stiles said, "I'm Stiles Gilmore, from down at JJ. Where can I find Mr. Le Queux?"

"Present and speaking," said Le Queux, suddenly beaming with hospitality. "Well, doggone. This a pleasant surprise. Get down."

Stiles dismounted, and they shook hands. "Have a chair," said Le Queux. "Have my chair."

"Not your chair," said Stiles. "This is fine." He sat on a nail keg against the log wall.

After a bit of introductory small talk, he told Le Queux about the telegram he had received, that the herd would be a little late.

"Makes no difference, no difference at all," said Le Queux. "How about a nice raisin cookie and a drink of cold well water? Or maybe something a little stronger?"

Before Stiles could answer, four men came around the corner of the building, four cowhands laughing and talking. One was runt-sized and skinny and turtle jawed, one was a messy looking kid, about fifteen, and one was stocky and leather faced, the typical foreman on any ranch. The fourth was Stiles' man with the bearskin chaps and the hairy arms. They came into view rolling as they walked, with the squeak of belts and the tinkle of spurs. They were absorbed in their talk.

Stiles got up from his keg and went forward to meet them.

When they saw him and saw the savage look on his face, they stopped, confronting him, perhaps ten feet away.

"You in the bearskin chaps," said Stiles, almost in a whisper. "Remember me?"

"Why, yes, I believe I do," said the man, pretending friendliness. "Ain't you the gentleman I see the other evening at Shaw's?"

"The same," said Stiles. "And the man you shot at in the dark later that night. And the man you followed across the mountains today, to try it again."

28

"Not me," said the man tautly. He cast his eyes about him at the others, as though Stiles were making a gross blunder. "What's this supposed to mean?"

"The man that was traveling with you," said Stiles. "Where is he?"

"They wasn't any other man. I come from Prentiss Creek alone."

"You better answer my questions. What was his name?"

"Listen," said the hairy man. "I come from town alone, I didn't shoot at you, nor nobody else in town, and I come back here by the way of the prairie, not the mountains. Ask anyone at Rankin's."

He was smoking a brown paper cigarette. Now he took the stub of it casually from his mouth and dropped it on the ground. In the same careless motion, he put out his foot and stamped on it. It was a common, natural action. Except that he used his left hand. His right hand swung back to his holster and grasped his gun butt. Stiles drew and shot him. He shot him twice, to kill. He was dead before he hit the ground.

There were the two thunderous reverberations, and then a moment of utter silence.

The faces of the three cowboys flamed with outrage and hate.

They backed up, separated, and took new positions. Their guns whipped into sight, covering Stiles in what could be a murderous cross fire. Stiles, his hammer at full cock, watched their faces.

"We goin' to kill you like a dog," said the messy looking boy. "That was a gunman's draw sure as hell. And we don't want no gunmen here at Q Cross."

"Suit yourself," said Stiles.

CHAPTER
FOUR

"Wait a minute there!" said Le Queux crisply. "Hold it!"

But the blood was hot in them, and Stiles saw it was touch and go. For an instant, Stiles wasn't sure whether they were going to obey their boss or not. In a split second, he could be on the ground, too, mouth open in a gout of blood, attracting flies.

Addressing Stiles, Le Queux said, "What is this all aboout?"

He was a different man now, painfully courteous, constrained. An autocratic gentleman. His manner said, you are a guest in my home and have performed an abusive act, but you must have an explanation for it, and I would like to hear it.

All of them, the cowhands, Stiles, holstered their weapons.

Patiently, Stiles retold his story.

The crooked-jawed cowboy said, "I don't believe I ever seen you in these parts before. If you're a stranger, how did you get across them mountains?"

"A man named Killigrew showed me the way," said Stiles He gestured toward the body on the ground. "Who was he?"

"One of my hands," said Le Queux. "Tom Shefield."

"Killed him and didn't even know his name," said the boy.

"He started his draw first," said Stiles.

"You scared him," said the foreman. "I'd have drawed first, too."

"And you'd have had just about as much luck," said the boy. "This man's a professional."

"No," said Stiles.

"He said your story was a lie," said the foreman. "He said they would bear him out at Rankin's. Did you ask at Rankin's?"

"I saw him like I said at the lake," said Stiles. "That was good enough for me."

"It ain't good enough for me," said the boy. "I'm going to ask at Rankin's. And it could be, if you're still around, I'll look you up and try you, despite that draw."

"I want no more of this squabbling," said Le Queux. "Pick him up and take him back to the tool shed, then bury him." They left.

When they were gone, Le Queux said stiffly, "I hate to admit it, but the truth is that Shefield had been worrying me a little lately."

"Worrying you, how?"

"He's been showing more money than I pay him."

"Maybe he'd been gambling."

"He didn't gamble."

"You mean robbery? You mean you think he was off now and then on the highway?"

"I doubt it. There's no stage line this side of the gap."

"What, then?"

"I have a feeling he was being double paid. I think he was taking my wages and some other man's too."

"What other man? And for what?"

"I wish I knew the answer to either of those questions," said Le Queux quietly.

Now his coldly restrained manner came back, intensified. Formally polite, he said, "Thank you for coming here to supervise the arrival of the herd."

"I want to be sure you're satisfied."

"Won't you stay with me here at my home until it comes?"

No invitation was ever given more formally, less cordially.

Just as formally, Stiles said, "I'm comfortable at the Minton House. And I'd better stay in town. But thank you."

Le Queux, bringing the conversation and the visit to an end, said, "Then I'll see you again, in a few days."

Stiles nodded, and mounted. From his saddle, he said, "What's this Rankin's they've been talking about?"

"It's a road ranch out in the prairie, just beyond the gap. You must have passed it on your way in."

"I came by the mountains," said Stiles harshly.

"Oh, yes," said Le Queux. "I remember now that that was what you said."

Stiles circled his horse, and rode from the ranch yard.

He was angry, but he was irritated, too. He had come all the way up from Texas to create a little good will here at Q Cross. It had seemed to him good business to have them strong behind him locally. And what had he done at Q Cross? He'd stirred up the cowhands into belligerent bumblebees, and even estranged Le Queux himself.

But he had stayed alive. He wasn't in the Q Cross tool shed, waiting to be buried.

He rode east. After a bit he passed through a thin scattering of fine looking cattle, and later, just at sunset, with the fiery orb directly behind him, tinting the bunchgrass to cinnamon, he saw the portals of the gap before him, two great low-hanging bluffs, first magenta in the sun's rays, then a streaky purple in the twilight. At the mouth of the gap, when he passed through it, he saw the grass change to greasewood.

He spent the night just east of the bluffs, in a shallow greasewood bowl cut by a meandering runlet from the foothills. He put his mare on long picket and went to bed early. Both he and his mount were tired.

He was up early, too, and on his way again in the predawn, before the sun.

This, he knew, must be Little Camas Prairie, and as day came he was impressed by the richness of the land. Nowhere had he seen grassland that was much better. This, he imagined, unlike the Q Cross pocket, was lonesome and endless.

It was still early in the morning when he first sighted Rankin's, and shortly afterward he was approaching it. Here, he had learned, were people who would lie for the hairy cowboy Shefield. He wondered if it was an outlaw rendezvous.

It was a flat square building, delapidated, on a flat, treeless plain. Where they had got enough logs and lumber together to build it, he couldn't imagine. A pencil line of woodsmoke rose from its stone chimney.

There was a wagon with an extra long bed and four sleepy mules at the side of the building, but no human in sight. Stiles dismounted at the rack. As he hitched his mare he glanced at the earth automatically, almost unconsciously, for a certain hoofprint, and found nothing. He would do this from now on, at every opportunity, hardly aware of his action.

He opened the door and stepped inside.

The room was not large and, despite the brilliance of the sun outside, it was dim and cool and loamy feeling. Through an open door at the rear came the cheerful sizzling of pork and skillet-browned potatoes. The place was empty except for a man who sat alone at a table in the corner, a youngish bleary-eyed man, stubble faced, clothed in greasy odds and ends, drinking whiskey from a tumbler. He lifted his hand to greet Stiles, and Stiles lifted his hand in response.

The floor was of packed earth, rock hard, and the log beams overhead had been squared, but roughly, with a broadax. A road ranch didn't have to be fancy. It was an emergency hostel. Customers who used it would be glad to get anything, as a rule, Stiles knew. There would be a couple of grubby rooms somewhere for any traveler who wished to spend the night, meals and drink would be available, and there would be a corral out back for, say, traders moving by with herds of horses. On the wall just inside the door hung a bull whip, property left by error, likely, by a passing freighting train. If freighting teams came past, a stage line probably did so, too, and the place was a stage stop.

There were four empty tables. As Stiles looked them over, deciding on a place to sit, the man in the corner said, "Why not sit here with me, if you ain't too proud?"

He was drunk before breakfast, and dirty as hell, but those things could happen to anybody. Stiles nodded, and joined him.

"Name's Winchester," the man said.

When Stiles eyed him, he said, "For a fact. Though most times I wish it wasn't. My, the things it makes people say. In Arkansas, where I come from, the Winchesters is a mighty big family."

"Is that so?" said Stiles politely.

A second man came into the room, from the door at the rear. He was about Stiles' age, and stripped to the waist. He carried a buckskin shirt in his strong teeth, a razor and a mirror in one hand, a lathered brush in the other. He set the mirror on a shelf pegged into the log wall, dropped his buckskin on the floor, and started shaving. When he had finished, he wiped off the remnants of dried lather with big, calloused hands, and donned his shirt. It was when he was putting on his shirt that they saw his belly and chest were laced with old silver scars.

Winchester said, "Why not sit here with us, if you ain't too proud?"

"Why not?" said the man in buckskin. "I got to sit someplace, don't I?"

As he sat down, he said, "I hope their chuck is better than their mattresses."

"I slept all right," said the stubble-faced man. "But, o' course, I ain't got good sense."

"I've slept better in the High Bitteroots," said the man in buckskin.

"You from that part of Idaho?" asked the younger man.

"Was, but never again. I'm a market-hunter and that was too far from a railroad. You can't make nothing. It drives up your cost too high. This fall I'm fixin' to hunt the Boises here."

A woman in a soiled apron appeared in the kitchen doorway, counted them, retired, and came in with heaping plates. She slapped it down before them, and left.

Wolfing the food from his plate, the man in buckskin said, "The food is even worse than the bed."

"Then don't eat it," yelled the woman, out of sight in the kitchen. "Just pay for it."

"Women are touchy," he said in a whisper.

"You're the first market-hunter I ever talked to," said Stiles. "They don't have them where I come from. How do you go about it?"

"You go up into the high mountains in the late fall," said the man in buckskin. "Just when the freezes are starting. Then you begin your huntin'. Elk, deer, fowl, everything. When you got a load, you cart it into the railroad. They fancy that kind of game a heap in the big Eastern hotels."

"How much do you get a pound for elk, say?" asked Winchester enviously. "My, the elk I've saw running around unbought."

"Sometimes they bring one price, sometimes another," said the man. "Like all market-hunters, I don't much care to discuss trade secrets."

He shoved back his empty plate, tossed a coin on the table, and walked out the front door.

Winchester chatted, and Stiles listened, relaxed and resting.

A little later, Winchester asked, "What did you make of our friend in Buckskin?"

"The market-hunter? He seemed to have a grudge against the world."

"And a lying tongue. If he's a market-hunter, I ain't."

"You're a market-hunter?"

"Sure am. That's my wagon out at the side. You hunt game in the mountains, some game, but not in the high mountains, unless you're bent on bighorn. And he wouldn't tell the price o' elk because he didn't know it. Game prices ain't trade secrets, for God's sake."

Now Stiles suddenly realized something. The man had gone outside, but there had been no horse hitched at the rack. He had spent the night. His horse must have been out back, in the corral.

Quickly, Stiles got to his feet. "You've done me a favor, I think," he said. "Let me buy you your breakfast."

"If you say so," said Winchester. "I'm a little short, right now, and thanks. Maybe sometime I can even pay you back with a nice juicy elk tenderloin, and maybe even quote you the going price, if you're interested. And I'd say watch out for that man."

Stiles dropped money on the table.

He left by the front door, circled the building, and came to the corral at the back. The ground by the corral gate was a mixture of hoofprints, old and new, but immediately he saw what he was looking for: a hind calk on a left hind hoof, with two significant dents in it.

Getting his mare, he returned and began his trailing.

This was the man at the lake, with his rifle at the ready across his saddlehorn.

Shefield's partner. Arranging an alibi, if needed, with the Rankins.

Or, more likely, Shefield's boss. His second, undercover, boss.

The stranger's tracks led Stiles northeast. By mid-morning, he was nearing the base of the bluffs he had just passed, and changed. The grass thinned, became arid and clayey. About noon, he found himself in an area of many crisscross little streams, dry at this season, some shallow bedded with flat banks, some deeply channeled, some with great mounds of eroded earth between them.

He wove his way in, around, over, and out, and the sign before him still remained clear and became fresher.

Then the hoofprints suddenly showed that the horse had broken into a gallop, and Stiles knew that he had been seen.

Then, all at once, by a tall loaf of dry earth, he was presented with a problem. Here, dividing, forking, were two sets of the same tracks. One set, a single set, the new set, went to the left; the other, many tracks there, coming and going, went to the right, descending.

He took the new tracks, to the left, and increased his speed.

In twenty minutes, he was in a land of stony alluvium and slab rock, and the trail and the man had vanished.

Patiently now, Stiles circled, quartered, and cast, using every tracking device known to the old hunters with whom he had grown up.

His quarry, in flight, knew the country better than he did. It was hopeless.

He retraced his way to the big loaf of earth, and followed the other set of tracks, to the right, down the slope. There were many of them, overlapping, and he strongly suspected that he was on the path to a cabin or hideout of some kind.

Before long, he saw that he was right. The slope leveled off, deep in a broad chasm of arid clay. The hoofprints clustered and ended here, with the sign of dung. Stiles dismounted, and saw bootprints.

These he followed to the chasm wall, around an upthrust tongue of clay, and found himself in a hidden chamber.

It was, he knew, what old-timers called a dugout. It was a lateral channel to the outside chasm, and its top had once been open to the sky, but was now covered over with green hides; above, on top of the hides, he knew, would be dirt placed there by the builder. Each side of the channel had been enlarged by shovel, forming a roomy, livable cave. There was a small heating and cooking range, old, but the wire that held its ascending stovepipe was glinting new. The floor was littered with mouldering bird and rabbit bones. There was a small cot, with two blankets and a buffalo robe on it in disarray, a short-legged stool, and a rust tin box with a cheap padlock on it. Prying the lock hasp easily with the stove poker, Stiles examined the contents of the box.

At first, the box seemed filled with clothes. On top of a pair of dirty drawers was a small heavy-iron implement, maybe four inches tall, shaped like a thick, blocky T; across the top of the T was a deep groove. Stiles laid it aside, and continued his search. More clothes, a half-woven horsehair hatband, a battered deck of cards, and a small blue bottle. There was a label on the bottle: *For Earache, Nitre & Rhubard, three times a day. Williamson Pharmacy, Prentiss Creek, Idaho.* Stiles had noticed the Williamson Pharmacy back in Prentiss Creek. He replaced things as he had found them, removing the bottle, however, and sticking it in his pocket.

Before he restored the stubby iron implement, he stared at it hard and long. He knew what it was, and had a good idea, in a general way, why the man had it. It was a swage, a tool that fitted into the slot in the top of an anvil, and was used by metal workers and blacksmiths. It could be used to make, or alter, a branding iron. He replaced it, and closed the box lid.

Stiles smelled rustling.

Now he had a good idea where Shefield, the hairy man whom he had killed, had acquired that extra money which had so disturbed Le Queux. But how did he, Stiles, come into it?

The old worry came over him again. He would feel a lot better when his herd had been delivered, and paid for.

He left the gullied brakes. An hour later, he was in Little Camas again, and headed south once more for Prentiss Creek.

The sere October grass became richer looking; soon he began seeing cattle, and good cattle, and not long after, he came to the ranch house.

It was a small ranch house, solitary on the vast plain, but it had a towering, expensive windmill. An elderly woman sat on the doorstep with a bucket of hot water, plucking a plump-chicken. Stopping a short distance away, not to alarm her, Stiles said, "Am I bound right for Prentiss Creek?"

"Yes," said the woman, and called, "Joe!"

A man appeared in the doorway. It was Killigrew, Stiles' guide and companion in the mountains. He beamed. "By golly. Get down."

Stiles dismounted. Killigrew said, "Ma, this is Mr. Gilmore, the young man I was telling you about. That owns the JJ down in Texas."

Mrs. Killigrew said warmly, "You're welcome here, Mr. Gilmore."

Killigrew asked, "How did you come out with the feller that was trailin' us?"

"There were two of them, it turned out," said Stiles. "The one you mean, the one I thought it was, come up to me when I was at Q Cross, and we got things straightened out."

"You had a little difficulty with this other gentleman?" asked Mrs. Killigrew, being motherly. "Well, I always said that if one human has a little difficulty with another human, and they treat it sensible, and each of them go halfway, they can accomplish wonders. Nice sensible talk will solve anything."

"Well, we got it worked out finally," said Stiles.

Taking her bucket and chicken, Mrs. Killigrew went to the back of the cabin.

"Marvelous woman," said Killigrew in admiration. "Lives in a world of ideals and chicken and dumplings. Let's water your horse, and go in and set, and give that saddle of your'n a little rest."

They sat in the little bedroom-parlor, talking mainly about cattle, getting to know each other better, and soon Stiles learned that Killigrew was secretary of the Middle Camas Stockmen's Association. It became evident to Stiles that while the Killigrews lived modestly, Killigrew was both wealthy and powerful in local affairs. Starting as a young man, buying footsore stock from emigrants, he now ranged his cattle in three separate areas. He was intensely impressed with the reputation of JJ cows, and asked many respectful and searching questions about Stiles' methods. After a bit, he changed the subject.

He said, "Them two fellows you said was following you in the mountains. I guess they meant no real harm after all?"

"They were trying to bushwack me."

"But you said you settled it with one of them?"

"I killed him. In the Q Cross ranch yard."

Killigrew's eyes went frosty. "What was his name?"

"Shefield."

"He had it coming to him," said Killigrew sourly. "I knew him, and never liked him. I don't want to pry, but would you mind telling me about it?"

"I've decided to tell you anyhow," said Stiles. "I figure I owe it to you. If there's something funny happening around here, you ought to know it."

Beginning at the beginning, he told him the whole story, repeating his mention of the shooting in Prentiss Creek, adding Billy Goodhue's telegram about the delayed herd, going into detail about the gunfight at Q Cross. Then he told about his breakfast at Rankin's, about trailing the stranger, and about finding the dugout and the swage.

"When you seen him at Rankin's," said Killigrew. "What did he look like?"

"Long jawbone. Pale-blue eyes. I saw him with his shirt off, and his chest and belly were covered with old scars."

"Them was cougar scars."

"You know him?"

"Know who he is. Name is Jim Maude. He's got a three state reputation as killer and cattle thief."

"Could Shefield have been working for him?"

"Had to be. I can tell you one thing. He wouldn't have been working for Shefield, not Jim Maude."

They sat for a moment, gazing at each other thoughtfully.

"I'm sorry to hear he's around," said Killigrew. "That could mean some good family man will be found in a lonesome gulch, half et by vultures. And his best cows missing. Jim Maude won't touch nothing but the best."

"You know something," said Stiles. "I can't get rid of the feeling that he's after my herd."

"The herd's on the trail, south of here. How would shooting you in the back, miles away, help him get it?"

"Then you don't agree?"

"Of course I agree. He has to be."

"Then what's he up to?" asked Stiles.

"This is cattle rustling country," said Killigrew. "By that I mean a heap more so than most. We got a lot of right kind of cows, and wrong kind of men. And the geography makes it a paradise for the thief. A lot of new ranchers is cow-hungry, still building up their herds, and when they're in that stage they'll buy a passel of stuff they'd look twice at when they're established."

"I hate to admit it," said Stiles, "but it's the same way in Texas."

"They's two shuttles. A little one, a tough little one, through the Boise spurs. And then the main one, up and back between Big and Little Camas Prairies. If you think Le Queux's boys are wild, and maybe they are, a little, you ought to see those cowhands up at the northern tip of Big Camas. Whoosh. And if Jim Maude steals your herd —"

"If Jim Maude *tries* to steal my herd," said Stiles, "he'll learn a little about Billy Goodhue and his Texas men."

"No offense meant," said Killigrew. "But Jim Maude has weathered many a good Texas drover before. As I was sayin', if he gets that herd, it's pretty sure to end up in the north end of Big Camas. And if it does, you may as well go home. Them Big Camas ranchers stick together, and don't care much what, or who, they kill. And if they once lay out good money for a stole cow, they sure ain't going to give that cow back."

Stiles looked grim.

Killigrew said, "And no one is going to make 'em give it back. Even a low-holster man from Texas."

"They don't have it yet," said Stiles.

"I'm just trying to let you know what you're up against."

"I know."

"I doubt it."

CHAPTER
FIVE

Stiles arrived in Prentiss Creek just at sunset of the next day, having camped out on the way.

Main Street was crowded with before-supper shoppers, townsmen, and cowboys taking it easy, standing around, looking at the townsmen and at other cowboys, enjoying an interval of city life. The courthouse, a temporary looking structure of whitewashed clapboard, sat back in a weedy lot, an American flag flying from its makeshift cupola. Two men stood by its front step and as Stiles passed they stared at him; from their suddenly stiff-lipped way of speaking he knew they were talking about him. He gave them a long hard stare in return, loading it with contempt because he didn't care for people who whispered about him, and continued on his way. He wondered who they were, and what they could be talking about.

After he had stabled his mare he went to the depot and asked if any more telegrams had come in for him. None had. He actually hadn't expected any; it was too soon, and Billy Goodhue had already said things were moving as they should. Except for the delay.

After he left the depot, he searched for, and found, Williamson's Pharmacy.

It was a little hole-in-the-wall place, smelling of herbs. Behind the counter was a girl about fourteen, dressed like she was about twenty, and wearing enough cheap jewelry to sink a steamboat. Stiles showed her the little earache bottle he had found in Maude's dugout, and asked her if she remembered selling it to him. She giggled, and said she hadn't made the sale, her father always handled the medicines. Her father was on a trip to St. Louis, Stiles learned, but was expected back any day.

She giggled again, and tried to sell Stiles some perfume, but he said some other time, and left.

Now that he knew Maude's name he no longer considered the bottle important, but he was a methodical man, and didn't like to leave any tag ends. He decided to come back after her father returned.

In the lobby of the Minton House, the clerk with the brass-rimmed spectacles greeted him warmly, took key Number 12 from the rack, and led him upstairs. In the room, as he was about to leave, the clerk said, "They'll be serving supper shortly downstairs. And I bet you're ready for it."

"A two-inch steak," said Stiles. "With four soft-fried eggs on top of it."

"You can't beat it," said the clerk. "That's the meal that won the West."

Alone, Stiles stripped, washed his upper body from the washbowl on the stand, put the bowl on the floor, stood in it, and finished his bath. He got a clean shirt

48

from his valise and put it on. He was about to go down to the dining room when there was a knock at his door.

He opened it, saw two men — one with a badge — and stepped aside. Warily.

The two men came in. Almost instantly, Stiles recognized them as the two men he had seen standing before the courthouse, whispering about him.

The man with the badge was tall, hunched, thin; there was scarcely any cavity at all to his eye sockets, giving a flattish look around his slotted eyes. He looked pretty tough. He said, "This is purely a social visit, Mr. Gilmore." He tried to smile, but his face wasn't made for smiles. "I'm Sheriff Gilpen. This is Mr. John Brannaman. A ranch owner from Big Camas."

"From the upper tip," said Brannaman. "Where they got all them owls and bobcats and gray wolves." He was about sixty, dried up from beatings of wind and sun, reptilian and predatory looking. He made Stiles think of a Gila monster.

"Mr. Brannaman is down here on a business trip," said Sheriff Gilpen. "He looked me up and asked me to bring him around and introduce him to you."

"Are you two gentlemen friends?" asked Stiles.

"Back in upper Big Camas, his brother-in-law is sheriff," said Gilpen. "I met his brother-in-law two years ago. I never had the pleasure of meeting Mr. Brannaman until this afternoon."

"I was just getting ready to go down and eat," said Stiles, not liking any of this.

"It'll only take a minute," said Brannaman.

"All right," said Stiles impassively. "Let's have it."

Brannaman said, "You are Mr. Stiles Gilmore, owner of JJ down south. Right? And your boys are bringing some cows north for Le Queux. Right?"

Stiles made no answer.

"If they are JJ cows, they're select," said Brannaman. "JJ cows is supposed to be the best. Are they making the trip in good shape?"

Stiles merely stared at him.

"How much is Le Queux payin' you per head?" asked Brannaman.

Ordinarily, this would be a harmless question. There would be nothing essentially secret about it. But this whole setup was strange, and somehow unpleasant.

"Ask Mr. Le Queux," said Stiles.

"I'm asking you," said Brannaman, suddenly vicious.

"Sheriff," said Stiles. "You brought him in, take him out."

"Let's go, Mr. Brannaman," said Sheriff Gilpen.

"Maybe sometime I'll have the mighty good fortune of running into you up at Big Camas," said Brannaman, "and can repay your hospitality."

They left.

So that was where the herd was due to wind up, Stiles thought. With a man like that. Well, Killigrew had said upper Big Camas was new range. And that probably meant that they could look forward to fine grazing.

He sat down on the edge of the bed, smoked a cigarette, and thought it over. He came up with nothing. The only thing he knew for certain was that any way he considered Brannaman, he didn't like him.

He got up and went down into the lobby, headed for supper.

He had circled the desk and was bound for the dining room when there was a touch on his shoulder. A gentle touch. He wheeled and saw the messy looking young cowhand of Q Cross, the youngster, who with two of his friends had been so bent on shooting him down in the ranch yard. There was a mat of glinting down on the kid's face, his checked gingham shirt was so soiled you could hardly see the design, and his boots had a lip of dried mud curled up over their soles.

He was smiling. He said, "Hold it, friend. No trouble. Teague wants to see you."

Stiles tood a moment, sizing the boy up. Finally, he asked, "Who is Teague?"

"Our foreman. You met him yesterday, out at the spread. You're supposed to come with me."

He walked across the lobby and out the front door and Stiles followed him.

The other two cowboys, the hardcase turtle-jawed man and the stocky foreman, were standing on the boardwalk, in the light of the lobby window. They had big grins on their faces, on the faces which had showed him so much hate such a short time ago.

Behind them at the hitching rack was a horse. One horse only, a big powerful black.

Teague, the foreman, said, "We want to apologize for the way we acted yesterday. Do you accept it?"

"I don't know," said Stiles. "I don't apologize easy myself, and I don't accept one easy, either. Why are you doing it?"

"Because Mr. Le Queux so ordered us," said the foreman. "And on our own, too."

"Why?" asked Stiles. "What happened?"

"The boy here tracks a little," said Teague. "After you left, Mr. Le Queux sent us back in the mountains, to see what we could find. Well, the boy found tracks just like you said, up at the lake."

"Tracks of how many horses?" asked Stiles. "Three?"

"Several," said the boy.

Stiles said, "Did you see a left hind print, with the hind calk dented a little?"

"I ain't no Indian," said the boy. "I just seen you was telling the truth."

"So I wasn't lying," said Stiles. "So now you're all smiling."

"No need to take it that way," said the foreman.

"Did you check on Shefield's story, too?" asked Stiles. "Like he claimed to have come by the plain and stopped at Rankin's?"

"No need to, after we seen the tracks," said the foreman. "Besides that Rankin place has a bad reputation. Nobody would believe what Rankin said."

"You were ready to believe him yesterday," said Stiles.

"Listen," said the foreman, getting a little taut. "You trying to start this thing all over again?"

"Take it anyway you want to," said Stiles quietly. "It ain't in me to forgive or forget when I'm set up for a three-to-one cross fire. You men were about to cut me down without a chance, and it wasn't you that changed your minds, it was Le Queux."

In a low, controlled voice, the turtle-jawed man said, "You don't care whether we part friends or enemies?"

"Not a bit," said Stiles. "I've had both before."

Now the kid said, "Mr. Gilmore, how do you like the looks of that horse?"

Stiles inspected the black at the rail. It was powerful, magnificent looking.

Stiles said, "It looks like one of the best."

"It is one of the best," said the foreman. "It's Mr. Le Queux's second favorite. We brought it in to Prentiss Creek for you. After you left Q Cross yesterday, after all that excitement, Mr. Le Queux said, 'Mr. Gilmore, so far from home and all, must be riding a third rate, rented, livery barn horse, and him used to the best.' He wants you to take the lend of it as long as you're up here."

"I'm sorry," said Stiles politely. "But I couldn't. Tell him thanks."

"Why not?" asked Teague.

"For one thing, it would be too much responsibility."

"Not with Mr. Le Queux.

"And for another," said Stiles, "I never like to be beholden to strangers, but maybe you don't know what I mean."

Surprisingly, Teague became thinly human. "Sure, I know what you mean. I guess I'm that way, too."

Stiles went into the hotel, into the dining room, and had his supper.

He ate at a little table in a far corner of the room. He'd finished his steak and eggs, and was working on a piece of apple pie, when a man appeared in the doorway from the lobby, and stood for a minute, surveying the tables. It was Mr. Rush, the Q Cross buyer. When he saw Stiles he came forward, sat down with him, and dismissed the waitress by saying he had already eaten. "I've been looking for you, Mr. Gilmore," he said. "They were saying you were back in town."

"Who was saying?" asked Stiles.

"Oh, Main Street," said Rush. "You know how it is." He offered Stiles a cigar, and Stiles shook his head. "Have a successful trip?"

"Yes," said Stiles. "I got back alive."

Mr. Rush waited for Stiles to elaborate. Stiles didn't.

Rush said, "I was just talking to Mr. Le Queux, outside of the barber shop. He says his men tell him you declined a fine horse he brought in for you."

Stiles nodded, and finished his last crumb of pie.

"Your refusal didn't offend him," said Rush. "As a matter of fact, I think it made you grow in his esteem. In the esteem of all of them."

"Is that so?" said Stiles noncommittally.

"May I talk to you as a friend?" asked Rush.

"Sure," said Stiles.

"I think Mr. Le Queux is growing to like you. I wouldn't be at all surprised when I visit you down south next year that I come to place an order twice as big as this year's. A really big one."

"Can I ask you a question, as a friend?" said Stiles.

"Why, certainly."

"Did Mr. Le Queux send you here to say that?"

Rush, unembarrassed, said, "Yes."

"First the horse. And now you with this flimsy bribe talk. What does he want?"

"A favor."

What kind of a favor?"

"That, I'm not permitted to say. He'll tell you himself. But it's one that is only to your mutual advantage."

Rush got up. He seemed to be sweating under pressure. Just before he left, he said, "You want to know something. You're a different man away from home. You're cold as ice. Fact is, you scare me a little."

Stiles didn't smile.

Rush left the dining room. His cigar had gone out.

After a bit, Stiles, too, left. He decided at first to take a little turn around the town, to become a little more familiar with it, but in the lobby he changed his mind. Dog tired he decided to go to his room and stretch out on the bed.

Le Queux was standing in the upper hall, just outside his door. His black broadcloth was dusty from travel. He had been riding hard, pushing it a little, Stiles decided.

He said, "Can I talk to you?"

"Of course," said Stiles, and opened the door.

They stepped inside, Stiles closed the door behind them, and pointed to a slat-bottomed rocker. Le Queux sat on the rocker, and Stiles sat on the bed. Examining his fingernails very carefully, Le Queux said, "They tell me you didn't much care for the mount I tried to lend you."

liked her fine," said Stiles. "It's just that generally
 ı̣ake it a practice of furnishing my own
transportation."

"I'm sure you do," said Le Queux. "I'm sure you go
through life that way."

Stiles remained silent.

"I like an independent man," said Le Queux. "He
doesn't ask favors. Trouble is, he usually won't grant
them either."

He hooked into Stiles with his eyes, and held him.
Impassively, Stiles said, "Try me and see. What's on
your mind?"

"Is this conversation in confidence?"

"You'll have to take your chances there," said Stiles.
"I won't even bother to answer that one."

Le Queux looked satisfied.

"First thing in the morning," he said, "I want to go
to the bank and draw out twelve thousand dollars in
gold. I want to buy those cows right now, immediately.
First thing in the morning, I give you the money, you
give me a receipt, and the herd is mine."

"While they're still on the trail? Before they've even
been delivered?"

"That's it."

"No," said Stiles.

"Why not?"

"That's not the way I do business."

"Give me one sensible reason."

"All right. I'm selling those cows to you because I
can make a profit. They cost me so much, and so much

56

only, per head to raise. You're willing to pay more than that."

"Naturally," said Le Queux.

"Say they were rustled on the trail, or something else happened to some or all of them. I'd have to refund to you the sales price, your price, the high price, instead of my price, the cost, the lower price. In other words, I'd not only lose the cows, but also, the margin of profit. Right?"

"No," said Le Queux. "Because I'd write out a little paper. An agreement stating I was taking the hazard. That you were in no way financially responsible."

"No," said Stiles.

"What's your objection now?"

"Paper or no paper, I'd feel honor bound to repay every penny of your money. And I'd do it, too."

Le Queux flushed with anger.

He said, "You're forcing me to tell you my side of this thing. I planned to resell that herd. And the buyer expected them right now. But because the herd hasn't shown up, and because he's a hot-tempered man, he might, for spite — he doesn't like me — start looking around for other cows to buy."

He waited a minute, and then continued. "If I could prove to him the cows were really on the way and a little late, and say they were traveling in fine shape, and show him a receipt or something proving I really owned them, then maybe I could talk him into holding out a little longer. He knows JJ cattle by reputation, and would much prefer them, but he's mighty hard to deal with when he gets his dander up."

Stiles made no response.

Le Queux got to his feet and walked to the door. The door open, his hand on the knob, he said, "I've scrabbled and scraped for every thing I've acquired —"

"So have I," said Stiles.

"I don't want to threaten you, but I'm a dangerous man to block."

"The answer is still no," said Stiles. "I got one way of doing business, and one way only. And that's not it."

"In other words, you are only interested in your deals, not mine."

Stiles said, "Goodnight, Mr. Le Queux."

CHAPTER
SIX

Next morning, after breakfast, Stiles paid the sheriff a little visit at the courthouse.

Now for an instant, but for an instant only, he really felt hollow for Texas. There were as many kinds of sheriffs as there were humans, and when you called on one it was always a big help to know just what kind this one might happen to be. Of course the best way was to have the sheriff your second cousin once removed, like Stiles had back home, but otherwise you had to take them as they were dealt.

Sheriff Gilpen was in his office, a little room at the back of the building scarcely larger than a cupboard, eating fried turtle and hominy which had been sent in on a tray from the saloon next door. His greeting of Stiles was friendly enough, but cautious. He twisted his thumb toward a chair, and Stiles sat down.

"I don't like to interrupt a man eating," said Stiles. "I can come back later."

"Think nothing of it," said Gilpen. "But if you'll excuse me, I'll just go ahead."

The sheriff chomped, laying down turtle bones meticulously, and Stiles sat impassive, his hands folded in his lap. He was being given the silent treatment, and he knew it.

Finally, the sheriff said, "After I left your room at the Minton House last night, I heard you killed that Shefield fellow out at Q Cross."

"I had to," said Stiles curtly.

"I heard that, too," said the sheriff. "This hominy has too much lye in it. Aiming to be around long?"

"Until my herd comes in," said Stiles. "Why?"

"Oh, I don't know," said Sheriff Gilpen vaguely. "There's just something about you that seems to steam off trouble. What was the scrap with Shefield about, anyway?"

"That's over and done with," said Stiles shortly.

"To what," said the sheriff, "do I owe the honor of this visit? Is they some way I can serve you?"

"I'd like to know a little more about this man you brought around to see me. This Brannaman."

"I don't know anything about him. Like I said, I was just extending the courtesies of my office."

"He asked some mighty prying questions about my trail herd."

"I thought so, too. But maybe that's just the way he is."

"Could he be mixed up with a rustling gang, do you think?"

"That's an interesting question," said the sheriff. "And it's all in what you mean, mixed up. Back up there where he comes from, rustlers is just people. I bet he's played checkers with many a rustler in his kitchen. But I've never heard no suspicion of him being a rustler himself, and these things get around. I'd just size him up as being meaner'n a pocketful of baby rattlesnakes. But for that matter, all the folks up there seem to tend a little that way."

"He was mighty interested in my cattle," said Stiles. "And he knew that they were already sold."

The sheriff said that hereabout, and even up in Big Camas, JJ cows had a fine reputation.

"In fact," said the sheriff, grinning, "an amusin' thing happened when that law business I mentioned took me up there a couple of years ago. I stayed with Mr. Brannaman's brother-in-law, the sheriff. At his house. He's a small rancher. While I was there, I seen three cows with blotched JJ brands."

"I didn't have JJ two years ago," said Stiles. "I'll check on the records when I get home. But I can tell you this, he didn't come all the way down to Texas to steal them."

"He didn't steal them at all, not himself," said the sheriff. "He bought them from a rustler, who might have got them in Wyoming, Colorado, anywhere."

"Maybe I'd better get into that upper Big Camas market myself," said Stiles dryly.

"Kin you sell as cheap as a rustler?" asked Gilpen.

Stiles shook his head, grinned, and left.

Out on the street, he thought it over. Since he had taken over JJ, he had made a careful study of its past ledgers. He could only recall one market for JJ cattle in southern Idaho, the Q Cross.

He wondered if those stolen JJ cows the sheriff had mentioned could have originated at Q Cross? Rush, Le

Queux's buyer, should be well posted on the ranch affairs out there. He decided to have a little talk with him.

Rush, in Levis, with a pitchfork in his hands, was in his grubby front yard, spreading manure, trying to prepare for a decent lawn the coming year. He looked up as Stiles joined him, weak eyed, pot bellied, pouchy jawed, and greeted Stiles pleasantly.

He looked and acted like the same old Rush, exactly, in every way, but suddenly Stiles had a strange feeling: that his presence wasn't welcome.

He had another sensation, too. A truly eerie one. That Rush didn't like him, and had never liked him. Caught off guard this way, surprised, it came and went across Rush's face in a flick, in the hot little pupil of his eye, in an unpleasant little muscle appearing and disappearing at the corner of his mouth. When he spoke, it was the same old voice, not honey and pancakes to cover up his dislike, but quiet, amiably, and dignified. He said, "Out for a little airing?"

"No," said Stiles. "I just wanted to ask you a question."

"Then let's go in," said Rush. "And sit down. I'll break out the old demijohn."

"Thank you, some other time," said Stiles. "It's this: has Q Cross, in the past, ever been raided by rustlers?"

Rush studied him carefully. "I don't mean to seem rude. But I can't see how this could possibly affect you in any way."

"It doesn't. I'm just curious."

"No," said Rush. "It never has. And I'd hate to be the rustler that tried it. Le Queux would run him down to the very gates of hell."

Stiles changed the subject. They talked for a while, easily, on diverse, inconsequential topics, and then Stiles said, "In Texas, most ranchers, except the biggest, do their own buyings. Back at JJ I don't see too many full-time buyers, like yourself."

"In the first place," said Rush, "Le Queux is a big rancher. He buys, sells, feeds, does just about everything. He has outside interests too. He is always up to his ears on affairs. He can mighty well use a buyer. And besides, my situation with him is a little unusual. I like the work. I went to him, and offered myself to him cheap, and he hired me. It gives me something to do, I get paid a little, and everybody's happy."

Stiles realized, all at once, that Rush was getting nervous. You could only tell it because he talked a little faster.

"I enjoy it," he said, beaming. "And that's what a man should do, what he enjoys. I travel a lot, here, there, everywhere, and like to travel. Got a little nest egg saved up. I was a small rancher myself, when I was young, before I was wiped out by the panic. Maybe sometime, moving around like I do, I'll see another small spread that takes my fancy, and buy it, and retire, and settle down."

"Yes," said Stiles gravely, and departed.

This talk with Rush stayed with Stiles all day, disturbing him.

That night, on his bed at the Minton House, he went over it again.

He wondered how big that nest egg of Rush's was, and if, like he said, he worked cheap, how he got it.

A strange idea kept coming into Stiles' head, and he kept trying to put it out, to dismiss it. It blackguarded Rush, and when you came right down to it there weren't any grounds for it, any grounds at all.

It was that Rush, the traveler, the buyer for Q Cross, could be working on the side for Jim Maude, the rustler.

It could be that Rush, under his respectable cover, moving around in the back country, could talk to questionable ranchers, cautiously, on the subject of stolen cows. If they seemed susceptible, he could push it. He could supply the customers, Maude could supply the goods.

Word could get around among dishonest ranchers, and a proposition like that could build up into a good thing.

He could even size up good herds for Maude to steal.

Why couldn't he in the past, for instance, have betrayed Q Cross itself to Maude?

They wouldn't steal from the Q Cross range. That might imperil their whole setup. But if Le Queux got a good herd, and sold it, Rush could pass the information on, and Maude could steal it from its new home. This could explain how Sheriff Gilpen had seen blotched JJ brands in upper Big Camas.

This, Stiles decided, could fit all the facts. Rush and Maude in partnership.

This would give Mr. Rush a nest egg, all right. And a nice big one.

But if this was so, and Stiles, going over and over it, could see nothing wrong in the reasoning, why had Shefield tried to kill him?

CHAPTER
SEVEN

He was awakened next morning by a faint tapping at the door, and opened it to let in Winchester, the market-hunter with whom he had eaten breakfast at Rankin's road ranch. It was a different Winchester, though, clear eyed, not drunk, shaved, clothes spick and span. Under his arm he had a package wrapped in newspaper. He handed it to Stiles.

Taking it, Stiles said, "What is it?"

"That elk tenderloin I promised you."

"Well," said Stiles, grinning. "Thanks. I'll get it cooked down in the kitchen."

"Then you'd better stand around and watch them cook it," said Winchester. "Cooks like elk tenderloin, too."

Now he handed Stiles a small folded piece of paper. Stiles unfolded it. It was a note.

Winchester said, "I come in on one of my uncle's horses. I got here just after dawn. I washed up in the back room of the barber shop. He said it was important to you."

Stiles was reading the note. It said:

Stiles, I have sent this man to you. He has something to tell you. You can trust him all the way. He is my wife's nephew. Killigrew.

Stiles began to dress. He didn't prompt his visitor. He knew better than to prompt a man carrying a message.

"After I left you at Rankin's the other morning," said Winchester, "I heard something. I heard that just before you and me and Maude met, he and some other fellows moved a herd."

"Where did you hear it?"

"From the Rankins. They're friends of mine."

"Moved it where?"

"Just past the road ranch, heading north. That's all they knew. He's done it before, they said."

"What brand?"

"It was at a distance. Just a cloud of dust."

"Then how did they know it was Maude?"

"He rode in for a bottle of whiskey," Winchester said. "And they sure as heck didn't ask him. You don't ask Jim Maude what brand he happens to be driving today."

It couldn't be his herd, Stiles thought. That would be an impossibility. The times wouldn't work out. They conflicted. His herd was miles south of Prentiss Creek. Not north of it.

"It seems to bother you," said Winchester.

"Yes," said Stiles.

Stiles didn't offer to pay him for the hardship of his trip. He knew better than that. This was a different Winchester. He tried to think of something he could do, or say, to express his appreciation. He wanted to wish him a good winter's hunting, but he knew better than that, too. Most hunters were superstitious, and some went by opposites. A good wish would be a jinx. Wish him good, and it would come out bad.

Stiles said, "Thank you."

"Glad to oblige," said Winchester quietly. "Uncle Killigrew says you'll do."

After Winchester had gone, Stiles went downstairs and had his breakfast. He seemed to have no appetite.

With his meal only half eaten, he got up, left the hotel, and went out onto the boardwalk.

He crossed the road, and entered the railroad station.

The stationmaster, glancing through a sheaf of freight bills, glanced up. "Good mornin', Mr. Gilmore," he said affable. "Can I help you? Care to send a wire?"

"No," said Stiles. "I was just wondering if anything else has come in for me?"

"No, sir," said the stationmaster.

"I really expected nothing," said Stiles. His trail boss would only have telegraphed at this stage, on the very last leg, if trouble had come up.

"If it's that herd of yours, you're thinking about," said the stationmaster, "forget it. You won't hear nothing more from it until you see it with your own eyes. The country it's in now, on its last lap, is out of this world."

Stiles left the depot.

The herd Winchester had told him about, the one Maude had driven past Rankin's, was another one, a second one.

It wasn't his.

It couldn't be.

He was walking down Main Street when he decided to talk it over with Killigrew. In the past it had been his policy to take care of his personal troubles himself, without outside advice, but this was a little different. He was a stranger here. He simply had to have a more complete, more detailed picture of the layout here, the local people and the terrain. Big trouble of some kind was in progress, and he was somehow in the center of it all. There was an alley between a saddle shop and a poolroom, an alley that led to the back entrance of the Minton House livery stable. He started down it, to reserve his mare for the trip. Tomorrow, he decided, would be soon enough. He decided, in fact, to reserve her for the duration of his stay. He should have done this before, he realized. She was a fine animal.

He was walking back up the alley, returning to Main Street, when he turned a corner and ran flush into a strange situation.

Teague, the Q Cross foreman, was standing in the center of the alley, arms folded across his chest, and Brannaman, the hardcase upper Big Camas rancher, was walking around him in tight little circles, looking him up and down insultingly, talking.

Teague stood sphinxlike, deadpan, bored. Brannaman was whispering at him hoarsely, working up a rage.

They both turned toward Stiles as he suddenly appeared.

Instantly, Brannaman began pouring out his bestial, insulting wrath on Stiles.

He said, "I didn't like you the other night, and I don't like you now."

Teague said earnestly, "Don't heed him, Mr. Gilmore. Keep walking."

Stiles shook his head. He came to a stop.

Brannaman, pushing his savage face a scant four inches from Stiles', mucous-crusted eyes, green scummy teeth, foul breath and all, said, "Shall I tell you why I don't like you?"

"Somehow, I don't much care," said Stiles woodenly. "Mr. Brannaman, I'm not going to take any more of your dirty abuse."

Teague said urgently, "He's got a wife and four children, Mr. Gilmore."

"He's got a gun with two notches on it, too," said Stiles.

Teague said, "Cool down, Mr. Brannaman. You're letting your temper rule your head. This man is a gunfighter."

"A dead gunfighter is just as dead as a dead polecat," said Brannaman.

"Mr. Brannaman," said Teague. "Next door to the courthouse is a saloon knowed as the Oasis. Go there, tell the barman I sent you, get yourself a quart of whiskey, and charge it to Q Cross. Before we're all sorry."

Brannaman stepped back and relaxed.

"If I start now, I'll drink all day. One quart won't do it."

Teague smiled. "Whatever you say. Just tell them Q Cross is behind you."

Brannaman, swaggering, left.

When he had gone, Stiles said, "Is he crazy?"

"No. Just loud-mouth mean. And he wasn't bluffing."

"I wonder how he got those two notches?"

"It could have been the long draw."

When Stiles looked puzzled, Teague explained, "Bushwhack."

"What was he onto you about?" asked Stiles.

"It was about that herd of yours Mr. Le Queux is buying. He was asking me all kinds of questions about it. And I wasn't answering."

"You know," said Stiles. "I don't like all this outside interest in my cows."

"Mr. Le Queux wouldn't like it either. And he would consider them his cows."

"I might be out in your part of the country in a few days," said Stiles. "Tell Mr. Le Queux I'd appreciate talking to him."

"Why not talk to him now?" asked Teague. "You'll find him in the back room of the feedstore."

"Where is that?"

"Just off of Main, on Congress Street. You can't miss it. Whenever Mr. Le Queux is in town, he spends most of his time there. He owns it. It's kind of a Prentiss Creek office for him."

They walked together to Main Street, where they separated.

On the way to the feedstore, Stiles passed Williamson's Pharmacy, and dropped in. There were two young girls discussing a dance with Mr. Williamson's teenage daughter behind the counter. It was about ten minutes before Stiles could break in. No, said Miss Williamson in answer to his question, her father hadn't come back yet.

He stepped out on the boardwalk to see the Q Cross hands who had just ridden by, Teague, the messy looking boy, and the man with the crooked jaw. They were in full regalia, warbags and all, and were obviously starting on a long trip, a trip longer than the one to their ranch. Stiles watched them till they turned from Main Street. They turned on Alder, which, he knew, left town southest.

Q Cross was north.

The sign, suspended by a wire over the dirt walk, said, *Grain & Feed. Cash & Credit.* Wagon scales of heavy timbers were set into the ground at the side of the building. Stiles crossed them, came to the building's rear, and entered a door. Teague had said "back room".

He found himself in a dingy office, almost as bad as a livery stable office. Nothing was as bad as a livery stable office, of course, but a feed and grain came close. The walls were grimy, the floor was stained with tobacco juice and littered with disgorged quids, and the one window had a broken pane patched with butcher's paper. In a feedstore you bought as cheap as you could, sold as high as you could, and saved evey penny. There was an open rolltop desk in a corner, its pigeonholes jammed with circulars and handbills, and in front of the desk, tilted back in a chair, was Le Queux. One elbow was on the desk shelf, and close by it was a big rat trap, all set and ready to go; rats were the plague of feed stores.

Le Queux was smoking a juicy looking cigar, in slow, delicate puffs, having himself a moment of meditation.

He gave Stiles a patronizing wave of the hand, to acknowledge his presence, and continued his silence.

Finally, just as Stiles was about to speak, he interrupted him. He said, "Mr. Gilmore, I've got good news for you."

Stiles held his speech, and waited.

Le Queux said, "I've sent Teague and two other hands to meet your herd, and help bring it back."

Stiles stared at him. "Why?"

"I've got a business to run. And I like to run it on schedule."

"Nobody can schedule a trail herd's arrival."

"I can't afford to risk any more delay."

"You mean your boys can get it in quicker than my boys?"

"Of course, and maybe safer, too. I'm doing you a favor. I should charge you for it, but I won't."

Black anger built up in Stiles.

"How a favor?" he asked.

"The last leg of a drive is always the hardest," said Le Queux. "The cows are tired, the drovers are tired. Your trail boss will be mighty happy to see a little fresh help ride in."

Stiles said, "My crew needs no help fresh or otherwise. When it does, it will ask for it, and it will ask for it from me, not you. At the moment, those cows are my concern, not yours, mine only, and their care is mine, not yours. Your interest in them begins when they cross onto your range, not before."

Le Queux hardly paid any attention to him. He said, "I've tried to deal with you, and you messed me up. Someone has to take charge here. When you come right down to it, though I hate to say it, I'm beginning to think that JJ is just simply incompetent."

After a moment, Stiles said softly, "Mr. Le Queux, I hope you are not going to regret this."

Le Queux looked at him, amused. He flicked an ash from his cigar, and closed his eyes.

Stiles swung on his heel and left.

In just about nothing flat, Stiles had saddled his mare at the stable and was heading away from town, southeast.

The crispness was back in the air again, and the sagebrush in the morning light was like a vivid ground haze. The autumn had been dry, and dust, so thin as to be almost invisible, hung to the horizon in a suspended golden vapor.

Finally, in the distance, he saw them.

A little later, they saw him, too. They turned their mounts, facing him, and waited for him to reach them.

When he joined them, they welcomed him with a smile of companionship. They thought he had come to accompany them on their trip.

"Turn around and go back," he said curtly.

Their air of comradeship left them. They looked unfriendly but amused.

"Don't tell me you're our new boss," said the kid.

"You heard me," said Stiles harshly. "I'm not going to argue."

74

He moved his horse around them, blocking their way.

"What's the matter with you?" said Teague. "Those cows are under contract to Q Cross. You don't own them."

"I own them," said Stiles. "Go back to town."

Suddenly, the cowhand with the crooked jaw looked pretty ugly. He said, "I take my orders from Mr. Le Queux, and him only. Move to one side. I'm comin' through."

He had the whole wide world to pass Stiles in, but he kneed his mount directly into Stiles', so that his horse's shoulder struck Stiles' mare at her saddlehorn. As the two animals collided, the cowhand gave his beast a rake of the spurs, so that it reared and hooves and fetlocks churned about Stiles' face.

Stiles caught the puncher's rein hand in a grip of iron, danced his mare back and to one side, and wrenched in cold fury, throwing his opponent from the saddle, dragging him beneath his own mount, trying in rage to dislocate his shoulder in the process but unsuccessfully. Then, instantly, his gun was clear of its holster and steady at his waist.

All the horses, even Stiles', went into a frenzy at the violent action at such close quarters, and it was an instant before they were quieted

When they had been controlled, the cowboy lay in a half daze, twisted on the earth beneath his horse's belly.

Teague swung to the earth, moved the mount to one side, and bent over the supine man. "You all right?" he asked in a hoarse whisper.

"I guess so." said the cowhand, staggering to his feet.

"Can you ride?" asked Teague.

The cowhand nodded weakly, and Teague put him into his saddle.

Only then, did Teague's attention come back to Stiles. He said, "I don't imagine any of us will ever forget this."

Stiles remained silent.

The kid said, "He could have been horse-tromped."

"Satisfied now?" said Teague, between drawn lips.

Stiles said, "Back to town. Or your trouble hasn't even started yet."

They gazed at him, as though he were a thing incomprehensible to them.

"I mean it," he said almost inaudibly. "Back."

They turned their horses and started back toward town.

He was sure that was truly where they were going, that they wouldn't try any tricks. He could see it in their faces as they left. And he could pretty well figure what they were thinking. Teague was thinking that this was a matter for the boss. The kid was thinking, Why die under a drawn gun, no-show, for thirty dollars a month? The cowhand with the crooked jaw was thinking, Wait, a better time will come.

He holstered his gun.

When they had diminished to specks in the northwest, he began his own return.

CHAPTER
EIGHT

His horse stabled once more in the Minton House barn, Stiles crossed the little back courtyard and entered the hotel through its rear passage. The clerk was behind his wicket in the lobby and Stiles, standing before him, said, "I wonder if I could have a word with you? Sort of in private."

"Certainly," said the clerk pleasantly. He closed a daybook, and left the wicket. "Let's go back here." Stiles followed him down the back hall, into a small, efficient looking office. They seated themselves.

Stiles had liked the looks of him all along, and now he checked him again, to satisfy himself. Tall, skinny, peaceful looking, in brass-rimmed spectacles and with sharp lynx eyes behind thick lenses. "I know your name, Mr. Gilmore," said the clerk. "But I doubt if you know mine. People hardly ever do. It's Harry Jordan."

Now, out of nowhere, really, the clerk had become a person, and a pretty fine one, too, Stiles was inclined to think.

"What can I do for you?" asked Jordan.

When Stiles hesitated, Jordan said, "I've had many and many a private talk back here. I've talked about overdue bills, about where to find a prostitute, about paregoric. Just about everything, But you stump me. Your problem is critical, but it is completely different. What is it?"

The thing that was worrying Stiles, really disturbing him, was that rustled herd Winchester had reported to him. The one driven past Rankin's road ranch by Maude. Even though he trusted this man Jordan, he was careful not to give him the details; for one thing, he didn't want to involve him.

Stiles said, "In Little Camas Prairie, up north of here, would it be hard to move a stolen herd?"

"Hard, yes. But a long way from impossible. If it was managed by a professional."

Mr. Jordan's voice was normal, conversational. But his eyes showed a quick glint of curiosity. The glint was instantly controlled.

Stiles sat a moment in thought. The rustlers that Maude had had with him, his helpers on the job, would more than likely be outsiders to the area. Strangers. Maude was an old-timer at his trade, a repeater. Local men, despite secrecy, would soon become known. Maude would certainly do what was customary in the trade: pick up new men for every new job. From Colorado, maybe, or Wyoming, or even Montana. They could be locals, of course, but there was too much danger in that; it wasn't probable.

Stiles said, "Say a crew of rustlers had a stolen herd up north of here, and sold it. What would they do then? Down in Texas they would separate, in ones and twos and threes, and get out to safe country."

"That's about what they would do here, too."

"All right," said Stiles. "We got them up north with their stolen herd. They sell it. And are loaded with money. Where would they go then?"

"They would scatter, like you say. And ten to one some of them, most of them, would dribble right back through Prentiss Creek, here. This is the bottleneck. Those prairies are enclosed on all sided by pretty rough mountains, and no towns for supplies. Of course they might choose the mountains, which I doubt."

"So do I," said Stiles. "Say a rustler on the run, loaded with money and feeling he was safe, hit this town. What would he do? Where would he go? I got an idea, but I'd just like your opinion."

"Now," said Mr. Jordan, a little icily, but pleasantly enough, "the conversation changes. You are inquiring about local citizens. About my neighbors and friends, in a manner of speaking. I have to ask you a few questions, for my own satisfaction. You are on the right side of the law?"

"So far," said Stiles, grinning.

"Cattle detective?"

"No."

"After these men for personal reasons?"

"I don't know. I think so, but I don't know. I've come to you in trust. If you don't think that you can trust me and my judgement, it's up to you and no hard feelings. You can get up and walk out."

Mr. Jordan nodded slowly. "That's good enough for me," he said. "We've got them here in town. Loaded with money, and hungry to spend a little of it. A woman named Emma Dinwiddie has a parlor house, across the alley just back of the jail."

"I doubt if at this stage they'd go to a parlor house. They're still moving, on their way out. And parlor houses are well known for prying into customers' businesses."

"They'd visit the saloons, of course. But that gets you nowhere. Everybody visits saloons. And as far as that goes, bartenders are close-mouthed. I don't like to run down my competition, but I can tell you another place they'd probably go. Shaw's."

"I hardly think they'd stay at a rooming house," said Stiles. "If they were hightailing. They might, of course."

"I mean Shaw's poolroom," said Mr. Jordan. "To relax and play a little pool. Most cowboys really got a weakness for pool."

"That's right," said Stiles. He got to his feet. "Thank you."

Mr. Jordan walked down the hall with him. He said, "It's none of my business, I know. But did they steal some of your cows?"

"I don't know," said Stiles. "I wish to hell I did."

He was going down Main Street, on his way to Shaw's poolroom, when he saw Sheriff Gilpen standing in the dust of the road by the wooden watering trough. There were three little boys, maybe ten or eleven years old, standing in front of him, looking up at him. As Stiles stepped down from the walk and joined the group, the sheriff said to the first little boy, "Worm him. When a hound-dog acts that way he needs wormin'." The boy walked away.

To the second boy, Sheriff Gilpen said, "Your ma's right and you're wrong. A double-yolked egg wouldn't necessarily hatch into a two-headed chicken." The boy left.

To the third urchin, the sheriff said, "You got a good idea, and I'll keep you in mind. Nobody would ever suspect a fifth-grader as a lawman. When I need sech a deputy, I'll write you a letter. That's a promise."

When this child, too, had departed, Stiles asked, "What goes on?"

"I've been holding sort of a Sheriff's Court, you might say. I get catched this way every once in a while."

"More towns should have a Sheriff's Court," said Stiles.

"You want to see me?" asked the sheriff.

"Yes, in a way," said Stiles. He told him about his fracas with the three Q Cross riders.

The sheriff listened attentively. At last, he said, "So you've come to me to file a complaint."

"No."

"What, then?"

"I just thought you'd like to know."

"Well, now I know."

"In my place, wouldn't you have done the same?"

"I can't seem scarcely able to put myself in your place," said Sheriff Gilpen, half in admiration, half in annoyance. "You're too overloaded for me."

"I'm not overloaded," said Stiles quietly. "I just stick up for my rights. And you know it."

The sheriff nodded, in sad agreement.

After a long thoughtful pause, the sheriff said, "You don't seem to get the picture. Mr. Le Queux is considered a dangerous man hereabouts. He mighty well could take this personally."

"So could I. He was messing with my herd."

"— He could mighty well take this personally. You just the same as slapped him in the face. If I was in your situation, I'd sweat a little. What's he going to do now?"

"We'll have to wait and see," said Stiles placidly. "There's more where that came from."

"Mr. Killigrew, from Little Camas, is in town looking for you," said Gilpen. "I take it it's nothing important. But keep your eye open."

Stiles nodded, and left.

There was only one entrance to Shaw's poolroom, through the rooming-house lobby. (It probably had its secret exits, Stiles decided, but that was a different story.) He opened the street door and entered. Again he was in the same dirty cubbyhole, pine-walled, plastered with sporting prints and semi-lewd magazine illustrations. Shaw, cadaverous and red-eyed, was again behind the counter. He looked up as Stiles came in, and there was a moment, Stiles realized, when Shaw tried to make up his mind whether to recognize Stiles or pretend he didn't remember him. He decided to recognize him, and said, "Why, it's Mr. Gilmore. How do you like our little town? I believe I heard you was staying at the Minton House."

"I am," said Stiles, "But time hangs heavy on my hands and I thought maybe I'd come in and play a little pool."

This sounded sensible to the proprietor, and he jerked a thumb to the open doorway at the left.

Stiles walked into the poolroom.

There were poolrooms, and poolrooms. He had once heard of a poolroom at St. Louis that was like a palace. This one was like a cave. There were four tables, but, at this hour, only two were being used. At first the disc lights on the worn green felt made vision difficult. Then, as his eyes became adjusted, Stiles saw the row of chairs along one wall, a drunk sleeping in one, a bright-eyed gnomish little man sitting in another, watching a lazy game in progress. The air was stale, reeking. All present, except the ball-racker, standing indistinct in a shadowed corner, and the gnomish man on the chair, were hard-bitten cowhands in range work clothes. The beer bottles on the table rails, the snick of the balls and jingle of spurs, was just as Western, just as much a part of a waddy's life as cookhouse beans.

Stiles went to an empty table, took down a cue, and looked around expectantly. The houseman, coming out of the shadows, appeared at his side. "I don't have anyone to play with," said Stiles. "I'll just play alone."

The houseman nodded, set the rack, lifted it from the triangle of balls, and walked away.

Stiles broke them, and began to play. He was no good at the game really, all his life he had been much too busy to work at it, but now he played his best. So he wouldn't look too inept, bogus.

A poolroom was like a club. It had its steadies, its day in, day out hangers on — generally small-time tinhorn sharpsters. It was a man like this whom Stiles wanted to talk to. A habitué.

Almost immediately, the gnomish man got down from his chair and joined him, watching ingratiatingly.

"My," he said, after a moment, "you're pretty good. You wouldn't want to play a game for small stakes, would you? But you'd have to go easy on me. I'm just beginning."

"No," said Stiles. "I'm just fooling around. I came here to talk to a man."

"Maybe I can help," said the other, eagerly, prying. "What man?"

"You," said Stiles.

"Not me!" the man said, in vague panic. He lived so touch and go, Stiles knew, that almost anything could stampede him. "I don't even know you."

"I'm trying to run down some cattle thieves," said Stiles frankly, to avoid palaver.

"Listen, friend," said the man softly, desperately. "I'm a pool sharp by trade. I wouldn't know a rustler if I seen one in the act of stealing."

Stiles held out his hand, in a fist, knuckles up. He turned it over, opened it, closed it, and put it in his pocket. A five dollar goldpiece had been cupped in the palm.

"How many were there?" asked the gnomish man.

"I don't know."

"What did they look like?"

"No idea."

"When were they through here?"

"In the last few days, I'd say. They had just made a sale up north, and were getting out of the country."

"Do you want to get my throat cut," whispered the man, "asking me questions like that, in this place? Yes, I seen 'em."

"All right. Let's hear about them. Do you want the money, or don't you?"

"Listen," the man said. "In a half hour, walk down Main Street until you come to the Busy Bee Bakery. They's an alley right beside it. Go down the alley, and you'll see a little privy that serves the merchants of that block. I'll be behind the privy, waiting. Half an hour, no sooner."

He departed.

For half an hour, Stile knocked the balls around on the table, then paid, and left.

The privy stood in a little quadrangle of hard earth, facing the back doors of a row of shops and offices. Also in the open space was a pile of rubbish as tall as Stiles' shoulder, a partially dismantled wagon, and a jumble of empty barrels and crates. The gnomish man was behind the privy, smoking nervously.

He said, "You're going to have to triple what you showed me."

"How do I know it's worth it?" asked Stiles.

"You're the judge. If it ain't worth it, don't pay me."

"Good enough," said Stiles.

"They came in drunk not long ago, late in the afternoon and played some mighty clumsy games of pool. One thing and another, and I got to talking to them. One of them, the drunkest, sure liked to argue. They come from Oregon."

"How do you know?"

"Drinkin' water. Every human thinks the drinking water he is used to is the best in the world. I said the best drinking water was right here in town. The argufier said, no, Oregon. And they all agreed. The argufier had some nice things to say about Jim Maude, the rustler, too. Does that give you what you want?"

"If they'd just come from a job with Maude, I doubt if they'd mention his name."

"Well, they didn't at first, I had to extract it from them, as us dentists say. Talking about this and that, I somehow got talking about cows and this seemed to lead to rustlers. It was when I told them Les Olliphant was the world's greatest rustler that the argufier got mad and said it was Jim Maude."

Intrigued, despite himself, Stiles said, "I never heard of Les Olliphant."

"That was my mother's maiden name. I just put it in to see what would happen. I guess I got a sort of sense of humor."

"What then?" asked Stiles.

"Then the others hustled the drunk argufier out."

"They didn't say what brand the cows had, or where Maude might be right now?"

"Do you think it's likely?"

"Because they mentioned Maude's name," said Stiles, "it doesn't mean for sure that they just came from a job with him. Maybe they just admired him. He has a big reputation."

"You wasn't there. I was. I seen how they looked and acted."

Stiles handed him two ten dollar goldpieces.

"Thanks," said the man, taking them. "And thanks for the extra five."

"That's for your tombstone," said Stiles amiably. "When you ask some future stranger one question too many."

And what did all this add up to? Stiles thought, as he made his way back to the hotel.

For one thing, it confirmed Winchester's story, added a few details to it, and brought it into sharper focus. Maude and his Oregon rustler-helpers had moved a herd up into Little Camas, all right. Now there was no doubt of it. But where it was now, or where it had been stolen, was still anybody's guess.

There were two ways, Stiles decided, that he could look at it. He could call it a local affair, concerning people who were strangers to him; he could say that it was none of his business, and forget it.

But was it a local affair? If it was a local affair, how come that he, Stiles Gilmore, was the storm center of so much trouble? He gets off a train, registers in a rooming house, and a man named Shefield, whom he had never heard of, tries to shoot him twenty minutes later.

And that was only the beginning. From there on, seemingly without purpose, he was faced with violence and crisis everywhere.

Badly overworked, he had, in a way, taken this trip as sort of a rest. Travel a little, he had thought, see some new country, shake a few hands, take a few drinks, make some new friends.

That's the way it had seemed, down in Texas.

CHAPTER
NINE

As Stiles came into the Minton House, Jordan, the clerk, told him that Mr. Killigrew was staying there at the moment, in Number 27, and had left word for Stiles to come up when he returned.

Number 27 was on Stiles' floor, at the end of the hall. Killigrew, barefooted, in pants and baggy underwear, welcomed Stiles mildly but warmly. He waved a hospitable hand toward the rumpled bed, said, "Care to stretch out?" and when Stiles declined and sat on a chair, stretched out himself, sighing in comfort. "Believe it or not," he said, "I ain't got no pressin' business in town. I jest come in to take a look at you."

"Well, how do I look?" said Stiles.

"You don't look fresh as a daisy, like when I first seen you," said Killigrew. "But you look reasonably alive, which is something to be thankful for, I guess. I hear you're still running around trying to pick fights."

"Not me," said Stiles. "I never picked a fight in my life. I just stand up for my rights."

He gazed fondly at the ferocious looking little man on the bed, the weathered face with its bushy gray moustache. He suddenly realized the depth of his affection for him. He had never known his father; he had been raised by his uncle. It was almost as though the man on the bed had come out of nowhere to fill this vacuum.

Killigrew said, "I was talking to some of the other members of the Middle Camas Stockmen's Association. I wouldn't be surprised if next year we got together a little money and sent down and bought a nice herd from you."

"That's the kind of news I like to hear," said Stiles.

"It ain't did yet," said Killigrew. "But it looks likely."

After a bit of talk about nothing in particular, Stiles brought him up to date on recent events.

When Killigrew heard about Stiles turning back the three Q Cross hands, he said, "You did the right thing, o' course. But you're sure as heck making enemies faster'n than I can eat a bowl of black-eyed peas."

Stiles then told him of his conversation with the poolroom sharpster, in the alley, behind the outhouse. About the three Oregon rustlers.

"That explains a lot," said Killigrew. "And my friends back in Middle Camas is going to be mighty glad to know about it. So that's where they been coming from. Yonder side of the Boise Mountains. That's what we thought, but it was jest speculation."

"But how could they bring a sizable herd *through* the mountains?"

"I don't know. I wouldn't like to try it."

"So now tell me what happened," said Stiles. "I got a pretty good idea, but I'd like to hear somebody else say it."

"Okay. A rustler named Jim Maude, with some helpers, steals a herd on the other side of the mountains — where they have some mighty fine cattle, by the way. He brings them through the mountains, into Little Camas and heads north with them. They pass the Rankin road ranch on their way north, like Winchester told you. I don't know where they'll finally wind up, but you can be sure it'll be way up in upper Big Camas somewhere."

"And this couldn't be my herd."

"In no way possible, I'd say."

"Then, when you come right down to it, it's none of my business."

"You know better than that, son. A stole herd, anywhere, anytime, is every cattleman's business."

"That's right," said Stiles. "I don't know what made me say a thing like that. You know I don't believe it."

"I know," said Killigrew. "You're under a strain."

On an impulse, he got up, dressed, patted down his wispy hair before the cracked mirror over the washstand. "Come to think of it, the story you jest told me, maybe we'd better tell it to the sheriff."

As they went down the hall, Stiles said, "What do you know about this sheriff? What kind of a man is he? I like him."

"That shows you got good judgement," said Killigrew. "They's only a few of us wonderful old-timers left."

He was a good twenty years younger than Killigrew, but Stiles saw no reason to mention it.

Sheriff Gilpen was in his chair behind his desk in his office, leaning back, smoking a pipe with a meerschaum bowl. He noticed them slowly, as though they were of no significance whatever, and said to Stiles, "If you care to associate with evil companions, son, that's yore business. But I'd be just as happy if you didn't drag none of this riffraff into my sanctum."

Killigrew said, "He's jest mad because we ain't come to bribe him about something. They say it's getting he won't talk scarcely to anybody anymore unless they offer him a bribe."

Stiles grinned and said, "Whoa." Then seriously, he told the sheriff about Winchester's report of Maude and the herd at Rankin's, about his, Stiles', experience at Shaw's poolroom and the talk he had had by the outhouse in the alley.

"Well," said the sheriff, disgusted. "Why bother to tell me? Even now. I'm just the leading county law officer."

"I didn't know anything for sure until now," said Stiles.

"And now you do?"

"I think we do," said Killigrew.

"Even if all this is true," said Sheriff Gilpen, "and the herd was stole, it's out of my authority by now." He tried to look relieved, happy. "It ain't no longer none of my business."

Killigrew said, "I swear, Charlie, you should make Mr. Gilmore here your deputy. His feelings run along with yours. Out of sight, out of mind."

Logically, aloud, the sheriff began to analyze the situation, and Stiles knew he was listening to a truly first-rate mind.

"I been hearing for sometime about ranches on the other side of the mountains," said the sheriff, and said it as though it were the other side of the world. "That they been losing select stock for quite a while. They been pretty sure, too, that it finally reaches upper Big Camas, but the man that goes back there inquirin' about rustled stuff had better kiss his wife goodbye before he leaves."

"Us stockmen where I come from think about the same," said Killigrew. "But they's one thing about the operation we can't understand. How do they get them through?"

Stiles asked, "How deep are those mountains?"

That was the question that bothered them.

"It's where you cross, of course," said Killigrew. "If they go in on the west side, and come out on the east side, just south of Rankin's road ranch, I don't see how it can be hardly less than eighty, ninety miles, wouldn't you say, Sheriff Gilpen?"

"And maybe more, if once in, they tried to pick easier going by traveling up and down between the ridges."

"I don't believe it," said Stiles. "Ninety miles of mountains."

"Neither do I" said the sheriff.

"Nor I," said Killigrew. "What's happening then?"

"There's something else," said Sheriff Gilpen. "The passes and valleys and sech, that give you the best way into the mountains, over there, have been suspected for some time. Folks keep an eye out. No one seems to see anything."

To Stiles, the sheriff said, "For a newcomer, you're turning out to be one of our most diligent countians. And we thank you for your cooperation."

Killigrew said, "He's got a sneaking fear that somehow this might be his herd."

"It can't be," said Stiles.

"But you'll be happier," said the sheriff, "when that herd comes in, and Mr. Le Queux hands over your money, and you're on your way back home."

"Well, naturally," said Stiles.

"You want to know something?" said the sheriff. "As much as I've come to admire and respect you, as much as I'll miss you, I'll be happier when you're on your way home, too."

Killigrew was careful not to smile.

Stiles said, "Let's go."

When they left the sheriff, Killigrew, pleading dust and fatigue from his trip, and saying he would like a little rest and a bath, returned to the Minton House. "I ain't as young as you," he said to Stiles. "Though I keep thinkin' I am."

Autumn night had come down over the town while they had talked with Gilpen and now Main Street, deep crystal blue under the stars, was deserted, empty looking. Stiles was leaning in the doorway of the Oasis Saloon, realizing in the excitement he had missed his noon dinner and feeling hungry, when a friendly hand took his elbow from the side, and Le Queux's voice, so jolly he didn't recognize it at first, said, "Let's go inside."

Stiles half turned, and there was Le Queux, all right, chesting up to him, squinty eyes, horse teeth, and all.

"I'll buy you your supper," Le Queux said. "It's the least I can do after our misunderstanding this morning."

Stiles allowed himself to be guided inside.

"Our misunderstanding?" said Stiles. "You mean you misunderstood me, or I misunderstood you?"

"A little of both," said Le Queux vaguely. "Anyone can make a mistake."

The Oasis Saloon was just a serious drinking and eating place. Two rooms were visible, the bar that they entered, and an ell off to the left where a part of a long boardinghouse type of table, filled with voracious eaters, could be seen. Behind the bar was a busy, florid man filling cardboard boxes with lunches which would be peddled sometime during the night on some passing train. Le Queux said, "What have we got tonight, John?"

"Chicken pie and buttered squash," said the busy man.

"Fine," said Le Queux. "We'll have two. In the back."

There was a door at the far end of the bar. Le Queux opened it; they went down a short hall and entered a sort of cubbyhole. Four chairs were pushed up to a table. On the table was a linen cloth, plated tableware, and an ornate kerosene lamp. "What the hell is this?" said Stiles.

94

"Deluxe, that's what it is," said Le Queux. They seated themselves. "It cost an extra seventy-five cents just to walk them fifteen feet to get here. I thought I'd give you a treat."

"Well, I'll be glad to eat and get out," said Stiles. "It looks to me mighty like a ladies' wine-room."

The barman brought in their meal, took his pay, and left.

They ate pretty much in silence. When they had finished, Stiles said, "Very good. Thanks."

He waited. He didn't crowd it.

Finally, as though the idea had just occurred to him, Le Queux said, "Martin Rush tells me that you two are pretty good friends, by now. Is that true?"

"I don't have many good friends," said Stiles. "I make friends slow."

"That would be my opinion, too," said Le Queux. There was brandy on the table. He took a sip, savoring it. Stiles left his untouched.

Le Queux said, "You know why he works for me?"

"Why, no I don't," said Stiles.

"Because he can't work for himself. His curse is drink. I mean, it's really a curse. So I took him under my wing and gave him a nice salary, and keep an eye on him."

"I imagine he gives you value received," said Stiles, not liking Le Queux's manner. "He really knows cows."

"Yes. But as well as I know him, he's a puzzle."

"I wouldn't know, and care less," said Stiles, trying to disengage himself from this kind of talk. He didn't believe in talking about anyone, personally, behind his back this way.

"He gets drunk sometimes, and talks a lot," said Le Queux. "Did he do it when he was down at JJ?"

"Ask him," said Stiles. "Don't ask me. I don't discuss my houseguests."

Rush had gotten drunk twice, and had done a lot of talking each time. What he had talked about was that he was the best cow buyer in the whole wide world.

"I'd like very much for you to answer my question," said Le Queux.

"And pay for my meal that way?" said Stiles stolidly. "No deal."

He pushed back his chair and got up. "Mr. Le Queux," he said, "in my opinion, a boss that tries to pump strangers about men that work for him is pretty bad."

Le Queux was completely undisturbed. He said, "I told you he was a puzzle. I don't like puzzles taking my wages."

Outside, something wet delicately touched his cheek. He held his sleeve to the light of a store window as he passed. There was a single snowflake on his cuff.

Mr. Jordan, the clerk, came out from behind his wicket as Stiles entered the Minton House, and intercepted him as he crossed the lobby headed for the stairs.

Jordan's face was bland but his glinting left eye behind its spectacle lens gave a slow significant wink. He said, "There's a horse back in the livery barn you may be interested in. A bay with a lame leg. Mention my name to the stableman and he'll tell you about it."

Stiles went down the corridor to the back court, crossed it, and entered the stable.

The stableman, a tough, seedy character with a chew of tobacco as big as an apple in the pouch of his cheek, came forward. Stiles said, "Mr. Jordan said mention his name."

"All right, you've did it," said the stableman, and waited.

"He said there was a horse here I'd be interested in. A bay with a lame leg."

The stableman took down a lantern, opened the back door of a stall, and showed the light inside.

Stiles simply saw a big bay. That and nothing more. He didn't recognize it.

"Where did it come from?" Stiles asked.

"A fella brought it in."

Groping for something of importance, Stiles said, "Why?"

"It went lame on him out in the prairie. Nothing serious, but it can't be rid for a while. I got the idea this fella was traveling in a hurry. He let me have it cheap, and bought another mare. We buy and sell too. I should make at least a hundred dollars on the deal when the bay's cured. That's how come I knew he couldn't wait, that he had to get gone."

"Ever see him before?"

"No, never."

"No idea who he was?"

"Of course I know who he was. He was Jim Maude, the rustler. With that old buckskin shirt they talk about."

Stiles lifted the bay's left hind leg. There was his old friend, the horseshoe, all right, it's hind calk worn, and nicked with those two little dents.

He replaced the hoof on the stall floor.

"Come and gone," said the stableman. "And long-gone, too, I'd say. That's his style."

CHAPTER
TEN

Killigrew had rested, and eaten, and was in Stiles' room waiting for him when Stiles came in. When Stiles told him about the lame bay in the stable, and wondered why Maude had brought it here, to the Minton, Killigrew said, "The Minton buys and sells high, and has a reputation of handling only the best. If I'd been in his place, in a hole for a good mount quick, I'd have done the same. You rush into a second-rate stable and buy a horse and you'll get ten miles out on the plain and be lucky if she's got enough wind to blow the spit out of her mouth. Where do you think he went?"

"I don't know," said Stiles. "But I'll find him. He's one man I want to talk to."

"You mean you're going to leave town?"

"If I have to."

"What if you find out he's somewhere up in upper Big Camas?"

"Then that's where I'll have to go."

"But why?"

"It's hard to put into words," said Stiles. He sat down angrily. "It's in my flesh and blood, I guess. I could never face myself again if this man, this scum, has over-rode me someway."

When Killigrew merely raised his eyebrows in sardonic awe, Stiles said, changing the subject, "There's another thing I can't get out of my mind. Brannaman. What does he really want?"

Killigrew got to his feet. Stiles noticed that tonight he was wearing his gun. "Let's go and ask him," Killigrew said.

"But where can we find him?" asked Stiles. He suddenly realized that Brannaman must live, must sleep, somewhere while in town. But where? "At Shaw's rooming house, do you think?"

"Shaw's is too high-toned for Brannaman," said Killigrew. "He'd be more at home under a green buffalo hide, behind a pile of manure."

"We'll work along Main Street, asking questions," said Stile.

"No need of that," said Killigrew. "I happened to hear from the postmaster today where he's quarterin'. Me and the postmaster was standing at his grocery counter, chattin', and Brannaman come in and bought a can of peaches and a sack of sody crackers. He acted so mean, even to the sody crackers, that when he left the two of us got to talking about him. He's living amongst the pigeon nests up over the Pastime Saloon."

Killigrew explained. The Pastime Saloon was the town's lowest drinking extablishment. The saloon was one story, but there was kind of a loft over it, which the bartender, who owned the property, sometimes rented to uncritical transients as lodging.

"I'll show you," said Killigrew. "Let's go."

"Maybe I'd better go alone," said Stiles. "There could be trouble."

Killigrew ignored him.

On Main Street, the Pastime, a grubby hole with green chintz tacked to the inside of its window frames, cutting out all vision from passersby, was separated from its neighbor, a harness shop, by an open passage, covered. Killigrew turned in and Stiles followed. At the end of the dark passage there was a door at the right, which Killigrew located by groping, and opened it. They climbed steep crude stairs which were little better than a ladder, and came out on a small landing with a second door. It was blacker than hell here, Stiles thought. Killigrew knocked.

The door opened, a man stood before them, stepping to let them enter, and they went inside.

The man was Martin Rush, the Q Cross buyer.

The loft behind him, sloping down on both sides of the ridgebeam to the floor, was lighted by a single candle. The candle was on a wooden box, and beside this was a smaller box for a chair. There was an army cot. On the floor in a corner was a pair of saddlebags, and a bedroll, Brannaman's likely. There was no Brannaman. No one but Rush.

Rush stood deadpan, with his back to the candle. Stiles said, "Where is Mr. Brannaman?"

"Out on the town somewhere," said Rush.

They could see he wasn't enjoying this.

"I shore don't mean to be personal," said Killigrew. "But what are *you* doing here?"

"Waiting for him to come back," said Rush. He was being careful not to offend them. "I have business with him."

"What business?" said Stiles, pushing their advantage. He had never seen Rush rattled before.

Abruptly, Rush got control of himself, and hardened. He didn't answer.

"Martin Rush has no business of his own," said Killigrew, as though he weren't even present. "He's the Q Cross agent. It must be Le Queux's business he's on."

"I didn't say that," said Rush, trying to leave the impliccation that it was true. "But I'll certainly report this meddling to him."

Actually, Stiles realized, this could have a very simple explanation. Nobody had said so in so many words, but he was pretty sure that Le Queux, the cattle dealer, had negotiated with Brannaman. To sell him, at a good profit, Stiles' herd when it arrived. Brannaman had come to receive it, but it was late. Brannaman, volatile, quick tempered, impatient, was becoming hard to handle. Le Queux and Rush were trying to hold him in line.

This was the simple explanantion, but many events had occurred that didn't quite fit the picture. Almost fitted it, but not quite.

"All right," said Stiles after a pause. "Let's move on, Mr. Killigrew."

As they headed for the door, Rush, maliciously, wolfishly, said, "You just might find Mr. Brannaman below. In the Pastime. On second thought, if you have

102

any personal questions, why don't you go down and ask them?"

"Why not?" said Stiles. "He asks some pretty touchy ones himself."

"Asks, yes," said Rush. "But would he enjoy the same treatment?"

"I believe we'll find out," said Stiles.

They went out of the loft, down the stairs and passage to the street, and entered the Pastime by its front door.

The room, long and narrow, floored, walled, and ceilinged with unplaned boards, reminded Stiles of an enlarged version of one of those box traps he used to make for rabbits when he was a boy. And that was about what it was, too, he decided. If you were a cowboy with a pocketful of pay, and entered that front door, and that door slammed shut behind you, you'd be here to stay, probably, until those pockets were empty and some master-hand released you.

There was a stubby bar along one wall, with a weasel-faced barman behind it, his nostrils and chin angry red with postules and sores. Three watches hung from the frame of the backbar behind him, taken in payment likely, and offered for sale, cheap. At the rear of the room was a battered circular dining-room table with a claw-and-ball pedestal; around it, in drunken concentration, sat three cowboys at poker, being carefully bellwethered by two tinhorn gamblers. Brannaman sat at a small square table midway along the wall across from the bar, a small glass of beer in one hand, a big free-lunch sandwich in the other. Across the table from him, facing him, was a big man with a bulbous face, a clean white dress shirt without a collar, and patched denim pants. These were all that were in the room.

Quietly, Stiles asked, "Know the man with him?"

Killigrew nodded. Scarcely moving his lips, he said, "Name's Blue. The town bully. Specializes in scarin' women and children. Claims to be a retired killer. Cross him, and he'll blow your head off."

"But he doesn't carry a gun."

"Dassent trust himself with one, he says. But get him mad enough, and he'll threaten to go home and get it."

"We got them like that in Texas, too," said Stiles softly. "Think they're talking over some kind of business together?"

"Heck no. He's just trying to cadge a drink. That's his real trade."

"He's wasting his time tonight," said Stiles.

He walked forward, and Killigrew sauntered along beside him.

"This Mr. Blue is a windfall," said Stiles almost inaudibly. "We can use him."

"How?"

"To soften Brannaman up a little, maybe. To show him we mean business."

When they reached the table, they stood before it, Stiles staring at its occupants. After a moment of pressure, he said, jerking his chin at Blue, "All right, out! Drag it."

104

At first Blue pretended not to understand. Then, ignoring them, flushing deeply, he said to Brannaman, "Are these friends of yours?"

"The sour looking old man I never seen before," said Brannaman. "The short chunky feller, I know by sight. But he's no friend."

"You heard me," said Stiles tonelessly. "Whip your tail out of here."

An incredibly insolent sneer came across Blue's bloated face. He kicked back his chair and got to his feet. "I'm goin'," he said, his voice loaded with menace. "But I'll be back. You just wait here."

To Killigrew, Stiles said, "What's he up to?"

Killigrew said, "Maybe he's fixin' to bring back a half dozen or so friends."

"I'm plannin' to bring back one friend, and one friend only," said Blue. "My .44."

Brannaman watched with interest.

Stiles said, "Maybe he can borrow a gun from the bartender."

"Oh, no, you don't," said Blue. "Just any gun won't do. I have to have old Sudden Death."

"Well," said Stiles thoughtfully. "This alters matters. He's spitting in our faces. He's threatening us."

"No, I ain't," said Blue, shaken. "I'm just statin' facts."

"Now I want to be *sure* he comes back," said Stiles. "Mr. Killigrew, you escort him home so he can get old Sudden Death, and bring him back. In the meantime Mr. Brannaman and I will have our little talk. Keep an eye on him."

"If I've give you gentlemen the wrong idee," said Blue, "I wish to apologize. I wasn't challenging anybody. I wanted to *show* you the gun. It's quite a curiosity."

Brannaman looked disgusted.

"Curiosity?" said Killigrew.

"Yes," said Blue. "It has walnut sideplates on its butt. They look like any other sideplates, but they ain't. Them sideplates was carved from the sleeper-log of the cabin where I was borned. I couldn't have challenged anybody." He held up a grimy thumb. "Look. I got a bone felon on my hammer thumb."

"I don't see it," said Brannaman.

"Well, it's there," said Blue. "Now if you'll excuse me, I'll be gettin' along. Good evening to you, sirs."

When he had left, Stiles, addressing Killigrew, said, "Now, I'm going to ask Mr. Brannaman some questions. I want you to listen to the questions and the answers, so if we're ever going into a court of law you'll be able to repeat them."

"Suits me," said Killigrew, looking suddenly hawklike, intent.

Brannaman, losing his usual bluster, looked confused and uneasy. "What is this?"

Stiles said, "When my herd comes in, and I get it on Q Cross land, and Mr. Le Queux pays me off, and it's then his property, is he going to resell it to you?"

"O' course not," said Brannaman, looking frightened.

What was there in this to scare him, Stiles wondered?

"Then the answer to that one is no?" said Stiles.

"Certainly, it's no," said Brannaman. "Where did you ever get such a idee?"

Stiles wondered, where, really, he had gotten it. Or rather, how. He'd gotten it from Le Queux, but had Le Queux actually named Brannaman as his red-hot prospective customer? Had Teague?

Brannaman said desperately, "I ain't in no market for no cows."

"You've been asking some pretty prying questions about that herd of mine."

"Is that so? I didn't know I was doing it. But it's only natural. Any stockman, whether he's in the market or not, is always interested in any cows. And JJ cows has a fine reputation."

"Know anyone else that's interested in that trail herd of mine?"

"Only Mr. Le Queux."

While Stiles thought this over, Brannaman said, "Look at this reasonable son."

"Reasonable?"

"Yes. Folks sometimes buys cows from Le Queux though they might cost a little more to save time and trouble and word, and because they's always good cows. Now back in upper Big Camas we're book ignorant maybe but we're used to work and we'd rather do the work and save the money. If I wanted any JJ cows I'd buy them from you direct, not pay no middleman his extra profit. That's reasonable isn't it?"

"I don't know" said Stiles. "Is it?"

He and Killigrew left the Pastime. Outside, Killigrew, tired, returned to the hotel.

Stiles, troubled, walked the streets trying to think it out.

Stiles was on the boardwalk before the Minton House, taking a goodnight breath of air before he went to bed, when there was a timid touch on his wrist. He turned. It was a girl. At first he didn't recognize her, then he remembered her. It was the teenaged daughter of Williamson, the druggist.

She said, "An earache is a terrible thing, my father says. He's just come home. He's tired, but he'll mix up that medicine for you right now." She started to walk, and Stiles followed her. He didn't bother to correct her.

Williamson, the druggist was waiting behind his counter. He was a stoop-shouldered man, sunken cheeked, and looked tired all right He smiled and said, "I hear you're in a bad way and want a little of my nitre and rhubarb."

Stiles cleared up the misunderstanding and said, "It's a little blue bottle, nitre and rhubarb like you say. It's very important to me that I locate the man that bought it from you. Can you give me any information?"

For ten minutes or so Williamson fussed through his ledgers.

Finally he said, "Here we are. I remember now. I remember the whole thing. The man's name was Bryce. He lived down at Swaynes Gulch."

The man's name was Maude, Stiles thought grimly. Bryce would probably be one of his many aliases.

"What did this Bryce look like?" asked Stiles.

"I've never seen him."

When Stiles simply waited, the druggist said, "The bottle was ordered and paid for by a traveling peddler, who often does such errand for his widespread back-country customers. This peddler is an old friend of mine, and we discussed the transaction over the counter here. He had never seen this Mr. Bryce either. A cowboy had stopped him out on the plain and given him the money and instructions."

"To deliver it to Swaynes Gulch?"

"Yes sir."

"Where is Swaynes Gulch?"

"South of here. Somewhere below the Snake. If I was you, I'd ask down there."

Back at the Minton House, he made arrangements for his coming trip.

"Everything will be ready for you," promised Jordan.

CHAPTER
ELEVEN

Next morning, after an early breakfast he started dead south.

Thick frost lay like powdered chalk on the dry dead prairie grass, but as the cherry disc of the sun climbed in the east and burned to pale gold, the frost vanished and the autumn air was like cider. Cindy, his mare, enjoyed it as much as he did. Now, after all these days, he felt that he was really getting somewhere.

Swaynes Gulch, he thought. Finally something definite.

Give me the name Swaynes Gulch, and a little time, and we'll be facing each other.

About five miles south of town he came to the river and an old building.

It looked like a very long rickety barn. Here and there its cupped siding was sprung from its joists, showing corroded nails like fangs, and its windows — there was a line of them, seven — were mainly glassless and boarded with rotting sagging frames. An apron of grass, now sere and yellowed, grew to its foundations. There was no one in sight. Beyond the building, down a slope, was a thread of alders and beyond the trees, the river lay flat and broad, studded with rocky islands.

Stiles hitched his mare to a rusty iron ring, one of a row in the building's siding, and called, "Anyone here?"

There was no answer.

He stepped inside and found himself in an empty room which had once been a store. Its walls were lined with bare shelves, littered with rat droppings and coated with dust; cobwebs hung like sun-moted nets from the corners of the ceiling.

But there was the scent of frying onions in the air.

He called again, and a man appeared in the doorway behind the counter.

He was a skinny man, bald headed, thin faced, with big spongy lips; his neck, though, was fat and encircled with pink wrinkles. He was drinking coffee from a soup bowl.

He said, "Had breakfast yit?"

"Yes," said Stiles.

"What can I do for you?"

"I'd like some directions," said Stiles. The man nodded. "Come back and have some coffee," he said.

Stiles walked behind the counter and followed him into a small, fairly respectable kitchen. He took a chair at a round table. The bald man placed a soup bowl of coffee before him, and sat himself opposite him.

Stiles came in on the subject obliquely. First he made a little small talk. "What place is this?" he asked.

"Years ago," said the bald-headed man, "long before the railroad was built up at Prentiss Creek, this-here was a ford on the old Oregon Trail. This is the crossing of the Snake, just behind us here. The trail used to come up on the southern side of the river, cross it here,

111

and then go on up northwest, past Boise. This is sorry land here, along the riverbank, but they's nice cattle country northwest, towards Boise."

"And this building was a store?"

"That's right. A big commercial supply station for passing immigrants, and when they got this far they sure needed it. Well, times changed, and it fell into neglect, like they say, and nobody wanted it. So I moved in. I don't have no title or nothing, and if anyone was to yell boo at me I'd move out."

Stiles smiled.

"The law calls me an untitled occupant. Other folks calls me a squatter. I call myself a sturgeon fisherman. They's some fine sturgeon upstream apiece. Now what's on your mind?"

"Know a man named Jim Maude?"

"He a friend of your'n?"

"What difference does that make?"

"A heap of difference. You might be a sheriff —"

"I'm not."

"You might be a sheriff, and me a friend of Maude's, so I'd tell you a lie. Or you might be a friend of his'n, and me an enemy to him, and he has plenty, so I'd tell you a different lie."

"Is that the only thing I'm going to get out of you, a lie?"

"I won't say that. But I will say this. I tell my share."

Stiles said, "I got an important matter to speak to him about. Relating to the cattle business. His style of cattle business, not mine."

That, Stiles decided, was vague enough.

112

But it wasn't vague to the man across the table. Swooping on it like a hawk, he said, "Stole cattle is his business. You mean you want to buy some stole cattle?"

"You'll have to figure it out yourself."

"Or they's another way taking what you said. Maybe he stole some cattle from you, and you're hunting him down to discuss it."

"My business with Mr. Maude is of a very personal nature," said Stiles. "It would be against my nature to go into it any further right here, right now."

"Doggone," said the man. "I'd sure like to hear about it. You don't know how hungry I git for gossip and excitement. To answer your question, yes I know him. He passes through here every once in a while, going both north and south."

"Could I find him right now down at Swaynes Gulch?"

"Might."

"Right now?"

"Oh, you mean right now? I couldn't say."

"How do I get to Swaynes Gulch?"

"That," said the man, grinning, "is general knowledge, and I can't see no harm in divulgin' it. Directly across the river from here is the mouth of a crick, now dry. You jest foller its bank south. You'll spend one night in the lava and get into Swaynes Gulch tomorrow. That lava's part desert, did you know that?"

They arose from the table. Stiles said, "I've seen deserts before. Not that I don't appreciate your warning me."

They left the kitchen, went through the empty store, out into the sunlight. Stiles mounted.

The bald man, studying him, said, "You got me a little mixed up, but I think you're decent at heart, so I believe I'll trust you with it."

He went into the building, and returned with an old army canteen. "One canteen won't do where you're goin'," he said. "Say your horse would lame and you'd be out in all that hell longer'n you expected."

Stiles took it from his hand. It was cool and wet. The bald man said, "I fought through three years of war with that canteen. Many is the time it saved my life. I love it like a brother, dearer than a brother. Because we got the same memories."

"Then I'd better not take it," said Stiles.

"Take it," said the bald man. "But drop in on your way back and return it. That's not unreasonable to ask, is it?"

"That was my intention anyway," said Stiles a little stiffly.

"Simmer down," said the man. "I meet all kinds. How did I know?"

Stiles circled the building, descended the slope, and crossed the broad shallow ford. In some places the water was only fetlock deep, in others it came up past his stirrups. His mare held steady, splashing delicately, walking unconcerned.

He found the mouth of the dry creek, and started south.

The terrain didn't seem too remarkable at first, but as the day went on, he entered into country such as he had never seen before, or even imagined. It simply seemed stark at first, but, as he got deeper into it, it became outlandish: patches of lava and greasewood and grass, but mainly lava, the grass scraggly and scattered. They'd called it semi-arid, but to Stiles it looked just plain arid. In the unsheltered glare of the sun, it was brutal, fantastic. It was a country of chasms and gulches and ravines, of lonesome monoliths and dead gray terraces, or rippled ancient pumice flow. In the distance, sometimes, in the hazy sun, he could see great bluffs of black basalt, like sentinels.

Steadily, he followed the creek bed in its wandering; sometimes south, east, west, even in short loops north. The wasteland became more desolate. He bordered trenches and canyons, passed great lumps of lava eroded to spiny backbones. Now and then, interspersed with this nightmare, there would be areas of tablelands, with grass. Grass in the main thin and scrubby, but sometimes not too sorry looking.

It was on one of these tablelands or meadows, if you wanted to call them that, this one quite large with good grass, that he came to the sheepherder and his wagon.

It was a typical sheep wagon, boxlike and weathered. The sheepherder's center of life and winter shelter, its sides now hung with domestic equipment and implements essential to his trade. A shaggy ungroomed horse grazed beside it, and behind it, in the distance, grazed the sheep flock. The sheepherder himself sat on a small step below the open taildoors of his wagon. He was mending a felt-topped boot.

He wore bib overalls and had a soiled red woolen scarf knotted about his neck. He had no weapon in sight but Stiles knew he could find one mighty quick, a rifle probably, if he should need one. Being a sheepherder, he lived in an unfriendly world, and realized it. He had a big ugly head and a tangled mane of ropey hair. All sheepherders were considered crazy by just about all non-sheepherders, and Stiles had to admit this one looked it.

They stared for a minute at each other, expressionlessly, then Stiles said, "Aren't you going to invite me down, so I can rest a little and talk a little to another human?"

"What have we here?" said the sheepherder. "Can it be the end of the world? A cowboy bein' polite to a sheepherder, and calling him a human?"

Stiles dismounted and sat on his hams.

A beautiful female collie, with liquid, intelligent eyes, came up and rested her bony chin on Stiles' kneecap. He scratched her behind the ears.

The sheepherder, highly pleased, pretended to ignore it. In their isolated, lonely lives, Stiles had heard, they had only two passions, love for their dogs and loyalty to their flock. And these emotions were so deep, they were beyond any outsider's comprehension.

After a long interval of silence, the herder said shyly, probingly, "Nice horse."

"Rented," said Stiles.

Silence again, and then Stiles said, "Nice looking dog. Fine looking sheep."

116

The herder looked pleased. "Oh, they ain't nothing much, none of them," he said modestly, his eyes gleaming happily at the compliment.

"How are you fixed for tobacco?" asked Stiles. "I got a couple of extra sacks in my saddlebags."

"Thank you kindly," said the sheepherder. "But I'm fixed fine in everything. I even got one third of a keg of whiskey. If I don't watch myself, I'm going to take a liking to you. By golly, I'll tell you what's let's do. Let's go on a three day drunk. Startin' right now, right this very minit!"

"I'm headed for Swaynes Gulch," said Stiles regretfully. "In a hurry."

"Swaynes Gulch? Why in the hell?"

"I'm looking for a man," said Stiles, suddenly feeling that he could trust this new friend.

"That so? Who is this man, if I might so inquire. You made a face when you said it."

"Name of Maude. Jim Maude."

"Oh," said the herder.

"Know him?"

"By hearsay only. The cow-stealing, sheep-hating son of a bitch."

"That's what I stopped to talk to you about," said Stiles. "How far is Swaynes Gulch? How do I get there? When do I get there?"

"You won't find him at Swaynes Gulch. If he was there, I'd know it."

"I have information to the contrary," said Stiles.

"I'd forget that information, if I was you," said the herder. "Somebody was trying to mix you up. Maude

117

never gets this far south. Why should he? Did you look for him up at the ford?"

"Up at the ford?"

"Sure. Every sheepherder in three counties knows that's his hangout. Baldy up there works for him."

Now Stiles understood the track about the earache medicine. The bottle had been put on the supply wagon, and, as a blind, directed to Swaynes Gulch. They knew the wagon would stop at the ford, on its way. At the ford, either Baldy, or Maude himself, intercepted it with some plausible excuse. That way, Maude got his medicine, and left no backtrack for inquisitive lawmen.

Stiles sat for a moment, thinking.

Then, he said, "So the ford is Maude's hangout?"

"One of them. It's just right for him."

"Just right? How?"

"Convenient to him. He raids them rich ranches up on the Oregon Trail, northwest of the ford, brings his stole cows down the west side of the Boises, and there is Baldy and his way-station."

Stiles mulled this over, and organized it.

So Maude didn't bring his rustled cattle through the mountain passes, as Killigrew thought. He simply skirted the mountains' southwestern edges.

"These rustled cows," said Stiles. "After they leave the ford, where do they go?"

"North," said the sheepherder. "North, up in the direction of the Camas country. That's all I know. Now you're gettin' way out of my territory."

118

Maude's cows came south, along the west side of the Boises, then veered north again, along their eastern side, certainly into upper Big Camas.

"Know something?" said Stiles, getting into his saddle. "You've made a friend."

The sheepherder said, "You're welcome here. Anytime."

Stiles turned his mare and started back, back to the ramshackle building on the bank of the Snake.

It was about nine-thirty, he estimated, when he reached the south shore of the river. There was a thin overcast of clouds in the sky, diffusing the moonlight, making the night about him smoky and indistinct. He could hear the gurgle and whisper of the water as it struck against rocky upthrusts, and see patches of white spume. He could not see the far shore, or even the old building, and decided that Baldy had put out his lights and gone to bed.

He touched his mare on her shoulder, and guided her into the water. There was danger here, he knew, of step-offs, and subsurface pits, but she made the crossing as calmly and sure-footedly as she had in daylight. As he approached the far bank, the old building began to materialize in murky blackness. Again ashore, with dry land under him, he tied his mare in the river-bank clump of alders and started up the slope afoot, walking silently.

When he came to the top of the slope there was still no sign of light in the building. He skirted it to its front, hugging its side, placing his feet unconsciously as his Apache friends had taught him long ago.

Despite his caution, he almost walked into a burst of lamp-glow.

At the front of the building, just around the corner, a window was open, with a light just inside, throwing a blossom of brilliant yellow illumination out into the night.

A voice was talking, and it was Baldy's. "Stop complainin' about that steak. It's so tender you could cut it with the edge of yore saucer. If it was any thicker, it would be a roast. It's the best steak you ever et, and you know it."

Maude, all right, thought Stiles grimly. Still griping about his food, like he had done at Rankin's.

He risked a glance into the window. At first he saw nothing. Then the bald-headed man was passing before him, back turned, with a coffeepot. Then there was nothing again, and Stiles withdrew.

"How could I have killed him?" asked Baldy, with a faint whine. "I ain't no pistoleer. And he sure as hell is. I've seen many a one. I saved him for you."

There was a hoarse grunt of agreement.

"It jest come to me whilst I was sitting looking at him," said Baldy. "I knowed you was on yore way here. So how, says I to myself, kin I git him back so you can take care of him?"

There was a moment of silence, and a rattle of knife and fork on china.

Baldy said, "So I loaned him this canteen, and told him some nonsense about it. And made him honorbound to return it on his way back. Which should be tomorrow late afternoon or early evening, I'd think.

Then you can do yourself what you been fault-finding me about."

Instantly, almost in the following breath, Baldy seemed to have turned into a lunatic. He said, "The most interestin' thing I ever had happen to me was this sturgeon I caught about three miles up the river, at Devil's Hole. It was bigger'n me. You know what I found in its belly when I opened it? A small softshell turtel, still alive, a mackerel, which is a saltwater fish, and a flint and steel which surely musta gone back to the old immigrant days. Being curious to see if it would still work, I took the flint and steel, and some dry sagebrush —"

Then Stiles knew he had been trapped.

For some reason, maybe because they lived suspicious tenterhook lives, they had become uneasy. Baldy, with his rigamarole, was holding his attention while Maude, probably through the back door, investigated.

Stiles slid out his gun and wheeled.

There was no one behind him.

Once more, he faced front. There was no one before him, either.

Or so it seemed at first. Then he saw the indistinct figure, like a shadowy alligator, maybe thirty feet away, crawling in the dark along the building's foundation. The man had come around the corner of the building on his belly, trying to get in a nice safe range. When he saw that Stiles had observed him, he shot. Three shots desperately fired, then, also wildly, a fourth.

He made a hard target. Stiles' first snap shot, a little off center, got him in the shoulder. Then, as he bucked up beneath the pain and impact, Stiles shot twice more and killed him.

Baldy came out the front door with a lantern. He said, "Did you get him?"

Stiles said, "Yes."

Baldy froze.

Together, they walked to the dead man.

In the lantern light Stiles saw it was not Maude, but Teague.

Teague, Le Queux's foreman.

"I brought back your canteen," said Stiles.

Wretchedly, the bald man said, "What you aimin' to do with me?"

"Start you running and shoot you down like a rabbit, I guess," said Stiles. "Give you a sporting chance."

He spoke casually, offhand, and tried to make it sound convincing.

Baldy flinched.

"Let's settle this peaceful," he said wildly. "I didn't want anything to do with them but they made me. You'd have did the same if they'd have come to you and laid down their orders."

"I doubt it," said Stiles, holstering his gun. "What were those orders?"

"I was jest to sit here and keep an eye open. They paid me for my food and grub. Until you come along, it looked harmless enough and a nice way to spend my old age."

"Keep an eye open for who? Law officers?"

"Oh no. I like law officers. Well, let's put it this way, I don't dislike them. Well, let's put it this way, I don't dislike all of them."

"Who was this 'they' that set you up in this nice business here?"

"Mr. Teague, the poor dead feller."

"You didn't name Teague just because he's dead and can't answer back?" After a moment's pause, Stiles said gravely, "I'm in no mood to listen to lies."

"I'm telling you the truth," said Baldy, and Stiles suddenly believed him. "That was what Teague was doing here, now. He come down to pay me my monthly salary. And ask me if I had any message from Mr. Maude."

"Were Maude and Teague friends?" asked Stiles.

"I couldn't say."

"Did they meet here often?"

"On occasion," said Baldy, looking tortured. "I must admit it, on occasion."

The revelation of this Maude-Teague relationship almost staggered Stiles. However, he pretended to be uninterested in it. He said, "The message Teague asked about. Had Maude left one for him?"

"I ain't seen Mr. Maude in a month."

"I've got a herd on the move, headed for Le Queux," said Stiles. "Were Teague and Maude planning to take it on its way up?"

"Oh, I wouldn't think so," said Baldy. Now he was the same old Baldy again, slippery, and full to the gullet with lies.

"Was Teague betraying his boss? Were they planning to steal it when it was on Q Cross range?"

"And try to outwit Mr. Le Queux? I'd say no to that, too. It would be too dangerous. Mr. Le Queux's a wildcat."

"All right. Say we've got the herd on Q Cross land. Mr. Le Queux is planning to resell it to someone, say. Teague would know who that someone would be. Could he have been intending to pass on the information to Maude, so Maude could steal it from its new home, the third party? This would leave Teague out of suspicion."

Stiles was just thinking aloud. He hardly expected an answer.

Baldy said, "Like I told you, they been meeting here for some time past. Maybe three years. That was long before you ever come into the picture, wasn't it? Why, certainly. So it ain't likely it's yore herd they was interested in at all, is it?"

Stiles made no answer.

"So if I was you," said Baldy, "I'd just ride on to Prentiss Creek and forget that part of it. And report Mr. Teague's sad demise to Sheriff Gilpen, o' course. I'll explain it to the sheriff."

"Saying what?"

"That you and Mr. Teague were lolling around on the ground together, restin', cleaning yore guns, highly sociable, and the tragedy happened. I'll have to shuffle that laying on the ground business in, because of the path of yore bullets, because you shot him when he was down. No offense meant, of course."

"And our guns went off. Quite a few times. All of his missing, all of mine hitting."

"Kin anybody prove different? I was an eyewitness."

Stiles shook his head in wonderment, turned and left. In the clump of alders at the river bank, he untied his mare and started back to town.

CHAPTER
TWELVE

A soggy blanket of cloud covered the stars, and there was an autumn mist in the air, not quite vapor, not quite rain, when Stiles rode into Prentiss Creek and stabled his mare. Main Street was dark and locked up for the night. There was, however, a single light in the courthouse, in the sheriff's office. As Stiles walked in, Sheriff Gilpen, asleep, his head on the desktop, nested in his folded arms, straightened, smiled and said, "Strange as it sounds, believe it or not, I got to do this because I got insomnia. Where you been?"

Stiles told him. He made a concise, detailed story of it, and ended with his shooting of Teague.

"I see," said the sheriff. "And by that I mean I don't see at all. Don't worry about it. If you did it, it had to be did. Your word is good enough for me."

"We wasn't laying around on the ground together, cleaning our guns, highly sociable," said Stiles grinning. "And I'd better so inform you, I thought."

"Now you or me could never work up one like that," said Sheriff Gilpen admiringly. "Most liars want to be believed and try to sound sensible. But old Baldy just doesn't give a damn."

"I think he told the truth for a minute or two there, when he was scared," said Stiles.

"Could be," said the sheriff. "Could possibly be." After a long pause, he changed the subject. "You missed the grand departure today."

"What do you mean?"

"Mr. Brannaman has went."

"Gone back to upper Big Camas?"

"I hope so, and so he told it all up and down Main Street, but I have an idea no. He said town life was too dull and expensive, both of which I'm sure he believes, so goodbye all. 'I cain't stand it no longer,' he said, 'I'm homesick for my ranch.' Him and his mount and his packhorse ambled out of town, north, about ten-thirty."

"I wonder what his business was here," said Stiles. "I admit that's a point that's been bothering me."

"It's been bothering me, too," said the sheriff. "The minute I met him, when he shook my hand and introduced himself, I asked him that very thing. He said he had just come to Prentiss Creek to look at a glass of real authentic government-taxed whiskey."

"And you don't think he's going home?" said Stiles.

"No, sir, I don't," said the sheriff.

"I don't see how you can tell."

"Before he left, he stocked up on provisions. When he'd gone, I went around to the store and asked a few questions. Among the stuff he had laid in was a sizable sack of dried beans. Dried beans either takes a long time to soak or a long time to cook. A man traveling as far as upper Big Camas would want to make at least reasonable time. Beans is camping provisions, not traveling provisions. He's camping someplace, waiting for something, I'd say."

"I'm sure you're right," said Stiles.

"But what is he waiting for?"

"The same thing he was waiting for in town, whatever that is," said Stiles. "He's just decided to pick a safer place to wait."

"But why, all of a sudden, did he move?"

"I must have made him uneasy some way," said Stiles. He told the sheriff about the scene in the Pastime the night before — it seemed a year ago — when he and Killigrew had confronted Brannaman and Blue. "My questions made him nervous."

"When questions make a man nervous," said Gilpen, "ten to one whatever he's up to ain't exactly legal."

All at once, outside, they heard a clatter of hooves thundering down Main Street, a single horse, being ridden by a lunatic, it seemed.

They both raised their heads and listened. "Some crazy cowboy coming into town," said the sheriff.

"Or leaving," said Stiles.

"A man that don't know no better than to treat a horse like that," said Gilpen, "should be forced to spend a week under a Mexican saddle with a sore mouth and a spade bit."

"Amen to that," said Stiles angrily.

He arose to leave. *I expected to make new friends on this trip,* he thought. *Well, I have. Three. Killigrew, Mr. Jordan at the hotel, and Sheriff Gilpen. As good as you could find anywhere.*

Smiling, he said, "Go back to sleep," and left.

Outside the sheriff's office, Stiles closed the door, and the hall around him became black, impenetrably black. Smells came to him, the ghosts of an empty public building, balsam and limey plaster, odors of human refuse, too, cast-off quids of chewing tobacco, sweat and body oil. When you were alone on a moonless prairie at night, you were really alone. But when you were in a dark, empty building there was always a residue of humanity at your shoulder. Stiles preferred the prairie. Nothing was visible in the darkness, walls, floor, ceiling, nothing but the big front door, open, perhaps thirty feet ahead of him down the hall. An oblong of smoky gray, with the misty night behind it, even it was scarcely visible.

He started down the hall towards it.

He had gone perhaps half the distance when a strange thing occurred. The figure of a man appeared in the doorway from the night outside, coming to a halt on the threshold, stopping. Stiles could hardly make it out, but he could make it out well enough to tell one thing. The man was standing with both hands above his head. At first Stiles thought he was watching a man in the act of being robbed.

Then, when the man spoke, and said, "I'm a friend. Don't shoot," Stiles knew the man had been waiting for him, and didn't want to startle him. Stiles removed his hand from his gun butt, and approached.

The rain had increased. As the man stood before him in the gloom, water running from his hatbrim and chin, it took Stiles an instant to recognize him. It was one of the Q Cross cowhands. The one with the crooked jaw.

The one who had been so malevolent when he had had his little fracas with them on the prairie south of town.

He was just the other way now, ingratiating, miserable.

"You know me, Mr. Gilmore," he said.

"I know you," said Stiles curtly.

"I seen you go in, and I been waiting for you," said the cowboy. There was relief in his voice. "You scare me. You notice I didn't jump out and say boo."

"Well, here I am," said Stiles.

"My name is Tom Luttrell," said the man, putting down his arms, but keeping his hands well away from his gunbelt. "Would it surprise you if I told you I was from Texas?"

"No. You sound a little Texas to me."

"Bastrop County."

"Yes."

"I'm tired of Idaho."

"I was myself a few days ago," said Stiles. "But I'm getting used to it."

"I've got to move on."

When Stiles simply waited, Luttrell said, "I said I *got* to move on. Without going into any details, I'm telling you I may get into trouble. Not yet, but I may."

"Is that what you wanted to say to me?"

"No," said Luttrell. "It's this. I'll make a swap with you. I'll do you a big favor, if you'll take me back to Texas when you go. And maybe give me a job with you. Any kind of job, at any kind of pay."

"What is the favor?" said Stiles.

130

Luttrell said mildly. "I don't horsetrade. I've made my offer. Do you want it, or don't you?"

"I don't usually hire men this way."

"Take it or leave it."

After a moment of intense thought, Stiles said, "Sold."

"You made the right decision," said Luttrell, exhaling a big breath. "You'll never regret it. Thank you. I think you'll find you've hired a moderate-good hand."

"And what was the big favor?" said Stiles dryly.

"A telegram come in for you this morning, and Teague, our foreman, went to the depot and got it and took it away with him."

Stiles was stunned. From whom? It couldn't have been from the trailherd.

He said, "Teague took it away with him?"

"Yes. But the stationmaster will have his copy."

"Did you see it?"

"No, but it happened just like I said. Teague told me."

Stiles looked through the rain, across Main Street's muddy rutted road, to the little railroad station. It showed light. The stationmaster was still there.

Luttrell said, "Do you consider that a big favor?"

"Yes," said Stiles, nodding vaguely. He took the path through the weedy court square, and headed across the road.

The rain was blowing a little now, swishing the puddles of the road in looping gusts. Behind him, the dark shop windows were filmed with running water, and doorways and alley mouths had dissolved into indistinguishable voids. Before him, across the road, was the little square depot and its platform. Here was the only important light in the area and its lamp was on the far side of the building, by the tracks, making the station itself seem cut from black paper.

He had almost reached it when a man stepped out on its platform from its far side, around the lighted corner, and faced him.

It was Jim Maude and his gun was in his hand.

Stiles never forgot the picture that flicked before his eyes. The long horsey jaw, the dull shadowed eye sockets, the wet buckskin shirt, sagging and shapeless.

The gun in Maude's hand was at full cock, his mind was set hair-trigger for kill, the element of surprise was with him. But the element of visibility destroyed him. He came from the light, and stood in the light, and Stiles had not yet quite emerged from the apron of shadows. It was that infinitesimal fraction of time in which Maude squinted, focusing, that wiped Maude out. Even then, the two men fired nearly at the same time.

Maude slammed around from Stiles' slug, crashed into the building beside him, and went down dead, his legs and arms tangled.

Death suddenly made his clothes seem too large for him.

The two shots, Stiles' and Maude's, roared out almost at one, and their reverberations had hardly pounded Stiles' eardrums when two new ones followed, thundering in the rain.

132

Stiles whirled. Behind him, coming from the boardwalk, now halfway across the road, a second man ran toward him, floundering in the mud, running like a maniac, shooting as he came.

Stiles killed him.

Steadily, as he would have killed a rabid dog.

He walked to him and turned him over. It was Luttrell. The man he had just "hired" to work down at JJ.

Stiles shook his head, as if to clear it of a bad dream. He covered the man's face with his hat.

Now two other figures appeared in the rainy night, from the direction of the boardwalk, Killigrew and the slovenly Q Cross boy, followed at a distance by Mr. Jordan of the Minton House. The kid was coming under Killigrew's command, being held on course with a rifle.

To Stiles, Killigrew said, "You want him? I don't. He was back in an alley yonder, taking a bead on you. When him and me is in town together, I kinda keep an eye on him. I know him of old."

The gunshots brought Sheriff Gilpen, who joined them. He handcuffed the boy. To Stiles, he said, "This is Irwin Johnston, knowed to his friends as the Ball and Chain Kid. He ain't much of a gunthrower, but he's been in more jails than you got fingers. I ain't been bothering him since he's been at Q Cross, because I thought he was making a clean start."

Stiles said, "You know something, Sheriff? That man we heard riding that horse like crazy. I bet it was Baldy, up from the south, bringing the word, the tip-off, on what happened down there."

"It was," said Jordan. "I was standing by the lobby window and saw him. Are you all right, Mr. Gilmore?"

"Yes," said Stiles. "Yes."

While they stared at him, he said, "Baldy brought in the word they were in trouble, and they set up a trap for me. It came mighty close to working. They stationed their men — trying to make it a sure thing — and Luttrell here talked me into walking into it. With a very smooth story, I might add."

Pointing to the dead man on the station platform, Sheriff Gilpen asked, "Who is that?"

"Jim Maude," said Stiles.

There was a moment of silence. Finally, the sheriff said, "My, my."

The kid spoke up.

He said, "Help me, and I'll help you. I always pay my way."

"The only way I'm going to help you, son," said the sheriff mildly, "is to keep you moderately well fed."

"Let's put it this way," said the kid, prison-wise. "If I talk, will you listen?"

"That's one of the things I'm paid for, to listen," said Sheriff Gilpen.

"I ain't going to take the weight of all this," said the kid. "And you can't put it on me."

"I cain't see how you have much choice," said the sheriff. "You're the only one left."

"If you don't stop him," said the kid, "he'll jest get him some new men, and set up the operation all over again."

"Who?" asked Stiles.

"The boss."

"Could you be referrin'," said Killigrew, "to Mr. Le Queux, the eminent rancher?"

"The eminent rustler," said the kid coolly. "Who do you think it was that Baldy reported to, that ordered Mr. Gilmore's death? It sure as hell wasn't me, or even Jim Maude."

"Where is Mr. Le Queux now?" asked Stiles.

"At the feedstore," said the kid. "Come on."

"I'm needed back at the hotel," said Mr. Jordan happily. "But this is a chance of a lifetime. Can I come along, Sheriff?"

"Sure you can come along," said Killigrew. "Can't he, Sheriff?"

"Glad to have you," said Sheriff Gilpen politely. "Glad to have you all."

"Jim Maude should be heavy with gold," said the kid. "You'd better search him before you leave him."

"I'll search both of them," said the sheriff placidly. "That's part of the usual procedure, son. It won't take long. And I always like to do it before witnesses."

"We'd better watch him close," said Killigrew to Stiles in a stage whisper. "That's how he lives like a king. Not serving papers. Dead men's pockets."

CHAPTER
THIRTEEN

Mr. Le Queux, in the back room of the feedstore, was in his easy chair by the battered rolltop desk, reading an Eastern newspaper in the light of a smoking kerosene lamp, when they trooped in. If the sudden visit bothered him, he didn't show it; and if the sight of the kid in handcuffs disturbed him, he didn't show that either. He was a mighty hard man to penetrate, Stiles decided.

Now Le Queux pretended to notice the handcuffs on the boy for the first time, and said, "Don't tell me you've been up to shenanigans, Irwin. You did right to bring him here, Sheriff. I'll go his bail."

"Irwin's shenanigans," said Sheriff Gilpen, "was joining up with Jim Maude and Tom Luttrell in trying to kill Mr. Gilmore. You must have heard the shots."

"Shots, shots, shots," said Le Queux. "Who pays any attention to shots in Prentiss Creek? I might have heard them. I don't recall. But one thing, I can tell you. My hands might quarrel, harmlessly, among themselves, but they wouldn't attack a stranger. Isn't that right, Irwin?"

"We was trying to kill Mr. Gilmore, on your orders," said the kid. "And I might add he got Maude and Tom."

Le Queux said nothing. He simply looked quizzical.

He figured out the outcome as soon as we came in, thought Stiles. *He's completely at ease.*

"I don't know what it is that you've really been up to, Irwin," said Le Queux paternally. "Strong-arm robbery, probably. That was your weakness, I understand, before you came to me. But whatever it was, you're a Q Cross cowhand, and I'll stand behind you. We'll bring in a good lawyer from Wyoming."

"You know something, Mr. Le Queux?" said the kid affably. "I ain't working for Q Cross no more, and I don't want none of its lawyers. All my life I've tried to go straight, and tried to go straight, and couldn't never seem to catch the hang of it. And I'm going to keep right on tryin'. The way I see it, a Q Cross lawyer would just be an extra handicap."

Killigrew grinned. Even the sheriff smiled faintly.

Completely unruffled, in low-voiced menace, Le Queux said, "I can't stand insolence from an employee. You're fired. I hope they give you twenty years."

"For jest holding a rifle?" said Killigrew. "He wasn't doing nothing but standin in an alley jest holding a rifle."

"All right, Irwin," said the sheriff. "You said you wanted to come here and talk. Or have you changed your mind?"

"I don't change my mind," said the kid through flat lips. "I'm just a sorry no-account, but, and it might surprise you, when I give my word I stick to it. Besides I never did like that outfit too much. They steal too big, and kill too easy."

Stiles said, "Back in the rain on the street, you said Mr. Le Queux was a rustler."

"He heads the operation."

"Then," said Stiles, "Why does he buy cows from me? Legitimately?"

"He doesn't lose any money on them, does he? JJ cattle is just like currency. Everyone in these parts knows he does this. He's supposed to be a dealer, and this helps him in his reputation."

"What was this operation?" asked Killigrew.

"Well," said the kid. "It was a pretty good one. It was divided in three parts, I guess you'd say. First was Rush. As a buyer, he traveled. He had a chance to spot good herds to steal, and also a fine chance to talk to crooked ranchers and find out in a roundabout way if they might be in the market for stole goods."

Stiles nodded.

"After Rush had lined up a nice herd, Maude and his helpers would rustle it," said the kid.

"I've never seen Jim Maude in my life," said Le Queux. "I've heard of him, of course, but never seen him."

"Why, Mr. Le Queux, you've seen him a heap of times," said the kid. "He always brought them herds straight to you, to get paid off. They was always held at Q Cross, until we, me and the rest of the hands, with Teague, delivered them."

"The Q Cross boys delivered them?" asked Mr. Jordan, who had been following this hypnotized.

"Yes," said the kid. "Sometimes we'd mess up the brand a little. We never said so in words, but sometimes we'd give the crooked rancher, say up in upper Big

138

Camas, a kind of idea that we'd stole them from Mr. Le Queux, our boss."

When no one spoke, the kid said, "We never had too much trouble unloading them. Mr. Le Queux has a high reputation as a dealer and Maude never took nothing but choice stock."

"Why did Shefield try to kill me the night I arrived in town?" asked Stiles.

"According to what Maude later told me," said the kid, "you scared the two of them when you showed up at Shaw's. They didn't know what you was up to. They did it on their own, following you and all, without Mr. Le Queux's orders."

"You know I believe the boy is telling the truth," said Killigrew. "All the way."

"So do I," said Mr. Jordan.

"What you believe, and what you don't believe," said Le Queux emotionlessly, "has no significance whatever."

"Who is Brannaman?" asked Sheriff Gilpen. "And what on earth was he up to?"

Slowly, the boy smiled. "Mr. Brannaman was almost too much to handle. He thought he was buying that JJ herd on its way up. He wanted that, and nothing else. And he wanted to see the bills of sale when he bought it. We had his herd waiting for him — one that Jim Maude had brought in from the other side of the Boises — but Mr. Le Queux couldn't fob it off until he had those papers to give me and Teague to flash at him. The more restless Brannaman got, the more nervous Mr. Le Queux got. You see, that was why Mr. Le Queux tried to send us down to hurry it up."

"Where is Brannaman now?" asked the sheriff.

"Out on the prairie, waiting. Waiting for the JJ herd to come in. So Teague couldn't show him genuine JJ papers and unload other cattle on him."

"These stolen cows from beyond the Boises," said Stiles. "Where are they right now?"

Le Queux tried to speak, failed, tried it again. He said, "I've been afraid of my hands. They've been tyrannizing me. I've been their tool. I have a bad heart. I had to do what they made me do."

"Ask Mr. Rush about that," said the kid.

"I will," said Sheriff Gilpen. "And about other things, too."

The kid said, "Mr. Le Queux tried to keep out of the picture, but he couldn't keep clear out of it. It ain't in him to do so. Mr. Rush should be able to tell you about bank accounts and such."

"Those stolen cows," said Stiles, pressing the point. "Where are they now?"

"Way up yonder on our northwest range," said the kid, "where we used to hold all of Jim Maude's stuff. At a place we call Hawk Butte Meadows."

"Is that right, Mr. Le Queux?" asked the sheriff. "I'm looking anyway."

Le Queux nodded mutely.

Shortly thereafter, with his two prisoners properly taken care of, the sheriff, with Stiles and Killigrew beside him, stood in the blustery night and knocked at Martin Rush's front door. After a bit, they heard the key rattle, and when they heard the lock-bolt click,

140

slipping back, the sheriff twisted the knob instantly and they pushed inside. Rush, cold sober and alarmed, stepped back and stared at them.

He wasn't a pretty picture. His face was rigid with fear. His robe was open and there was a little eyebrow of hair that ran from his pigeon chest down to his globular potbelly. He said, "It's all over, hey?"

"Yes," said Killigrew.

Sheriff Gilpen said, "Get some clothes on."

"Where's Mr. Le Queux?" asked Rush.

"In Cell 2," said Sheriff Gilpen. "Waiting for the court to sit next spring."

"What are you going to do to me?" asked Rush.

"Put you in Cell 3, and watch over you," said Sheriff Gilpen. His face grew red and seemed to expand. "Here I'm getting along nice and quiet with a few drunk and disorderlies, and a few disturbings of the peace, and a few chicken stealings, and now this. I've been a sheriff for twenty year, and this is going to be my worst winter."

"How is that?" asked Stiles.

"If you think it's all over, you're wrong," said the sheriff. "Word is going to get across the Boises, to the ranchers who have been abused by these prisoners. And these same ranchers is going to get together with a few of their friends, and make the ride to Prentiss Creek, even if the snow is withers deep. And when they get here, you know what they're going to want to do?"

"What?" said Rush, sweating.

"They're going to want to borrow Mr. Rush and Mr. Le Queux, just for a little while, just for an afternoon, just for a trip out onto the plains. Naturally, I can't lend them, and there's going to be vilification and bad language, and maybe even deeds."

"I'm a state's witness," said Rush, bug-eyed. "I'm going to testify for the prosecution."

"Is that so?" said the sheriff, interested. "Of course, I can't offer no threats, nor inducements, nor enticements, nor anything like them, but I'm sure the prosecutor will be happy to hear that's how your inclinations runs."

A week later, Stiles and Killigrew sat in an alcove of the Minton House dining room, eating a late breakfast of steak and eggs.

It had been a mighty busy week. Stiles had stayed in town, but Killigrew and Sheriff Gilpen had ridden out to Q Cross, to Hawk Butte Meadow, and found the stolen cattle. On the way out they had learned from Rankin's road ranch that the countryside was well informed of the shootings and arrests. They had learned something else there, too. That Brannaman had stopped in for supplies, traveling supplies this time, and, greatly agitated, had headed north.

"He's lit a shuck for home, for real, this time," said the sheriff. "I doubt if anyone could ever get him out of his county again."

After finding the rustled cows, and sending a Camas man in to watch them, Sheriff Gilpen had come straight back to Prentiss Creek to notify their owners. Killigrew had broken his trip back with a day at home.

142

Now, having just gotten in to town, and eating this second breakfast of the day as sort of a celebration, he said, "Looking at it from your point of view, everybody wins but Stiles Gilmore."

"That's right," said Stiles.

"What are you going to do with your JJ cows when they come in?"

"I don't know," said Stiles. "I never heard of anything like this happening before. A herd delivered, and no one to receive it. Hold a sacrifice auction, I guess. It's going to do me damage, serious damage, but they can't be moved around and home again. That's a fact."

"You could rent grazing for them, and winter them over," said Killigrew, "and peddle them next year in twos and threes and such, to butchers maybe, and homesteaders."

Stiles looked aghast. "I'd rather destroy them for their hides and tallow."

Killigrew laughed. He puckered up his eyes and opened his mouth. No sound came from him, but he was having the laugh of his life.

"I stopped off on my way back to town," he said. "And had a little powwow with some friends o' mine, fellow members of the Middle Camas Stockmen's Association. We got up a little pool together. We'll buy them JJ cows of your'n, and gladly, when they show up, if you'll give us a little time on them. This is sort of sudden for us. We'd have to have until a year or so to pay."

When Stiles could speak, he said, "I ought to give them to you. After all you've done for me."

"Until next year, then?"

"Until eternity."

"That's a little longer than we'll need," said Killigrew. "But thanks."

Sheriff Gilpen loomed up and took a chair at the table with them.

"I've got a crow to pick with you," said Killigrew.

"Then pick it," said the sheriff.

"It's about Irwin Johnston, the kid," said Killigrew. "I never liked him much before, but I seem to like him a little now. Not much, but a little. You owe him a lot, and you know it. Couldn't you get the judge to go easy on him?"

"I could," said Sheriff Gilpen. "But the kid would take it as an insult. He pays his way. He don't want to be beholden to nobody."

When neither Stiles nor Killigrew said anything, the sheriff said, "I think I will. Talk to the judge, got him two months, and two months only. If I should get him two months, when he gets free, Mr. Gilmore, would you give him a job? He'd need a job."

Stiles blinked. He shook his head no. The kid was incurable. "I'll never hire a hand away from home again," he said. "Luttrell taught me a lesson."

"How about you?" the sheriff asked Killigrew.

"Now you know I'd like to," said Killigrew. "But the way us folks works up where I come from, we seem to have all the help we need."

"We'll give him that short sentence anyway," said the sheriff, smiling.

"I'll tell you what I will do, though," said Killigrew. "I'll get up a little purse for him, when he gets out, to leave the county on."

"Good enough" said the sheriff. "I know he'll appreciate it. It'll give him something to throw away in Shaw's poolroom before he leaves."

The sheriff arose. As he was about to leave, he said to Stiles, "You owe me two dollars."

Stiles handed it over, looking puzzled.

The sheriff explained. "They was this fellow come up to me in the Oasis a time back, and asked me to buy him a bear, saying you'd make it right to me. I kind of got the idea that he expected it."

"A two dollar beer?"

"He wouldn't drink it out of nothing but a milk bucket. He was good enough to ask me to join him, but I politely declined."

Stiles amused and yet annoyed, said, "What was his name? What did he look like?"

"He looked terrible. And he said his name was Billy Goodhue. Claimed he'd just finished a trail drive, or something similar, for you, and had the cattle just north of town. He said he was looking for you. Of course, I didn't believe that trail-herd part. If so, as well as you and me has got to know each other, how come you never thought to mention it?"

"You know how it is," said Stiles. "It just slipped my mind."

Billy Goodhue came in through the door and pushed his way past the tables.

He was carrying a skinful, and for real. But where some men, drunk, got noisy or gay, Goodhue, who rarely drank, became cumbersome and ponderous. He was a big man, moon faced. His clothes were travel-worn, grimy with groundin dust. The arm of his jacket was ripped from thorns and an inch or two of the stitching was unraveled along the side of one boot. He sat down heavily, with a thud.

"Stiles," he said in a gravelly voice. "It's been a hell of a drive. How you been?"

"Never better in my life," said Stiles.

They grinned at each other, in deep, silent comradeship.